Praise for
Jessica Sorensen

The Destiny of Violet & Luke

"Gripping and heartbreaking . . . You will be hooked,
and you won't be able to not come back"
ReviewingRomance.com

"Sorensen's intense and realistic stories never cease to
amaze me and entice my interest. She is an incredible writer
as she captures the raw imperfections of the beautiful and
the damned"
TheCelebrityCafe.com

The Redemption of Callie & Kayden

"I couldn't put it down. This was just as dark, beautiful,
and compelling as the first [book] . . . Nothing short of
amazing . . . Never have I read such emotional characters
where everything that has happened to them seems
so real"
OhMyShelves.com

"A love story that will overflow your heart with hope.
This series is not to be missed"
UndertheCoversBookBlog.com

Breaking Nova

"*Breaking Nova* is one of those books that just sticks with
you. I was thinking about it when I wasn't reading it,
wondering what was going to happen with Nova . . . an
all-consuming, heartbreaking story"
BooksLiveForever.com

"Heartbreaking, soul-shattering, touching, and unforgettable . . . Jessica Sorenson is an amazingly talented author"
ABookishEscape.com

The Temptation of Lila and Ethan

"Sorensen has true talent to capture your attention with each word written. She is creatively talented . . . Through the mist of demons that consume the characters' souls she manages to find beauty in their broken lives"
TheCelebrityCafe.com

"An emotional, romantic, and really great contemporary romance . . . Lila and Ethan's story is emotionally raw, devastating, and heart wrenching"
AlwaysYAatHeart.com

The Forever of Ella and Micha

"Breathtaking, bittersweet, and intense . . . Fans of *Beautiful Disaster* will love the series"
CaffeinatedBookReviewer.com

"Powerful, sexy, emotional, and with a great message, this series is one of the best stories I've read so far"
BookishTemptations.com

The Secret of Ella and Micha

"Heart-breaking, heart-stopping and heart-warming and I couldn't put it down once I started reading"
onemorepage.co.uk

"A beautiful love story . . . complicated yet gorgeous characters . . . I am excited to read more of her books"
SerendipityReviews.co.uk

The Ever After of Ella and Micha

JESSICA SORENSEN

sphere

SPHERE

First published in Great Britain in 2014 by Sphere

A CIP catalogue record for this book
is available from the British Library.

ISBN 978-0-7515-5531-8

Typeset in ITC Garamond by Palimpsest Book Production Ltd,
Falkirk, Stirlingshire
Printed and bound in Great Britain by
Clays Ltd, St Ives plc

Papers used by Sphere are from well-managed forests
and other responsible sources.

MIX
Paper from
responsible sources
FSC
www.fsc.org FSC® C104740

Sphere
An imprint of
Little, Brown Book Group
100 Victoria Embankment
London EC4Y 0DY

An Hachette UK Company
www.hachette.co.uk

www.littlebrown.co.uk

To my readers, this one's for you.

Acknowledgments

A huge thanks to my agent, Erica Silverman, and my editor, Amy Pierpont. I'm forever grateful for all your help and input.

To my family, thank you supporting me and my dream. You guys have been wonderful.

And to everyone who reads this book, an endless amount of thank-yous.

The Ever After of
Ella and Micha

Chapter One

Micha

I'm trying not to think of all the messed-up reasons why Ella wouldn't show up to our wedding, but it's fucking hard. After everything we've been through, she didn't even call or leave me a note. My thoughts keep drifting back to the day after we kissed on the bridge and how afterward she told me that she loved me. I'd gone over to her house the next morning, ready to talk about it—talk about us—hoping she hadn't changed her mind overnight, after she'd sobered up.

When I climbed up that tree and ducked into her room, all I found was an empty bed. She was gone and that was worse than just dealing with an Ella in denial over her feelings for me. I knew she loved me even if she wouldn't admit it, and I could handle that if it meant she was still in my life. But having her gone, missing from my life, having no idea where she was,

was like losing my arm—or my heart. And right now, I feel like I'm verging on that that place again.

The cab driver is moving at a snail's pace down the road that leads to the secluded neighborhood Ella and I have been living in and it's driving me crazy. He actually looked at Lila, Ethan, and me like we were the ones who were insane when we'd hopped into the cab and I told him to drive as fast as possible, not worrying about the speed limit.

"Can't you drive any faster at all?" I ask, thrumming my fingers on top of my legs. "We're barely moving."

He shoots me a dirty look through the rearview mirror. "I'm driving the speed limit."

"You say that like it's okay," I say, leaning forward toward the plastic window dividing the front of the cab from the back.

"Micha, relax." Lila touches my arm, trying to calm me down. Her blonde hair and red dress are damp from her jump with Ethan off a cliff into the ocean. They were having fun while we waited for Ella to show up. We should all be having fun. But now I'm being stood up.

Stood up. Shit.

I slam my palm against the plastic, losing my cool, something I rarely do, but all I keeping thinking about is that she ran. Again. "I swear to God, you need to press down on that gas pedal or else—"

"Micha," Lila hisses, her blue eyes firm on me as she grabs my arm and jerks it away from the plastic window while the cab driver narrows his eyes. "That's not helping."

I rake my fingers through my hair and then undo the top button of my shirt because it's suffocating me. Lila hits redial on her phone, trying to call Ella for the hundredth time, but it goes straight to her voice-mail. Ethan's hardly said anything, but I know what he's thinking—that I should have expected this. Except that's the thing he doesn't get. Yes, Ella does this kind of stuff a lot but it's because she's either scared or confused or hating herself. It's what she's done since we were kids. I know this, just like I know that no matter what, we'll end up together.

Finally, the cabbie pulls up in front of the small single-story house I've shared with Ella since earlier this year. I don't even bother waiting for the car to come to a complete stop before I shove open the door. I toss a few bills through the slot in the window and stumble over my boots as I step out onto the curb. Ethan shouts at me to settle the hell down, but I shrug him off and jog across the lawn, stomping over the flowers tracing the path to the front door.

I remember when we first came to look at the house. My mom knew a Realtor in San Diego and she

3

said she could hook us up with a cute house we could rent for dirt cheap, due to the fact that the owner was an old woman who bought it back when houses were affordable. Ella and I had taken our time wandering around looking at the small bedrooms, the narrow but decent kitchen, and the wide backyard. I could tell Ella was pretending that she was uninterested, but I could see it in her eyes that she loved the house.

"So what do you think?" I'd asked, nudging her with my shoulder as she stared at the yellow shutters decorating the front of the house.

She'd nonchalantly shrugged, but bit her lip, which meant she was trying to suppress her enthusiasm. "It looks like a house."

I moved up behind her and wrapped my arms around her waist, stifling a smile as I dipped my mouth toward her ear. "A house you could see yourself living in?"

She dithered and then amusement laced her voice. "Well, me, yes, but you I'm not so sure. Maybe we'll have to find another place for you. Or better yet, you could always live in the garage."

I pinched her ass and it made her squeal. "Don't pretend like you're not picturing all the many places in it that I could fuck you," I whispered hotly in her ear.

She shuddered and I knew right then that it would

be our first home. We moved in a week later and everything has been going good for the last six months. I've been working on recording an album in a small studio near here, playing in concerts with a lot of musicians who are similar to me, playing anywhere we can just to get the chance to play while Ella works at an art gallery and goes to school, wearing my engagement ring on her finger. She seemed happy and even content when we decided it was time to actually have the wedding. I'll admit I would have rather had it back home where my mom could come to it, but Ella and I decided we'd have the wedding here, just she and I, and tell everyone later because it seemed to make Ella more at ease about the idea of getting married. It wasn't really a big deal to me, not to have anyone there but Ella, me, Ethan, Lila, and the minister. I mean, I haven't talked to my dad since I gave him my blood and marrow, so I wouldn't have even invited him to begin with. But I know my mom's going to flip when she finds out we got married without her…or she would have flipped anyway. Now I'm not so sure there's even going to be a wedding.

Shaking the damn thought from my head, I make my way to the house. I unlock the front door and hurry inside, scanning the living room for a sign that Ella's bailed. Everything looks normal, but then again, when she ran the first time, she barely took any of her stuff.

I go to the back door and check out the grassy yard and deck, but both are empty. My hope is dissipating as I walk past the empty bathroom and into our bedroom, the pressure in my chest building at the thought that she's gone. *She left me. Shit.* But when I push the door open, I jump back, shocked by the sight of her. She's sitting on the bed, overwhelmingly gorgeous in a white-and-black wedding dress, her legs pulled up to her chest, her chin resting on her knees, her auburn hair pinned up in tangled curls. The bottom of the dress is pulled up over her feet, revealing that she's wearing black combat boots, not heels like a lot of girls would. It almost makes me smile because I couldn't picture her looking more perfect and more like herself if I tried.

But when she looks up at me, her big green eyes filled with so much sadness, it rips the approaching smile off my face. I don't say anything as I make my way to the unmade bed, maneuvering over the pile of discarded clothes, sketchings, and my guitar, and then I sit down beside her. Reaching forward, I sweep strands of her auburn hair out of her eyes and tuck them behind her ear, then trace a line with my finger up and down her cheekbone. I wait for her to speak first, because I don't know enough about what's going on in her head to know what the right thing to say is.

We sit for what feels like forever, staring at each other, and the longer it goes on the more nervous I get about what she's going to say when she finally does speak. I hear Ethan and Lila walk up to the door, talking under their breath, but the sounds of their voices quickly fade as they leave right away, like they sense that we need to be alone.

"I'm so sorry," Ella says, finally breaking the silence. She lets out a deep sigh as she peers up at me through her eyelashes, biting her bottom lip.

I fight the urge to close my eyes against the sting in my heart. "What happened? I thought..." I cup her cheek with my hand, telling my unsteady voice to shut the hell up. "I thought we both wanted this."

Her bottom lip springs free as she releases it, then she lifts her chin off her knees and sits up. "We did... I do... It's just..." She releases a frustrated breath and flops her hands against the mattress.

Pressure releases in my chest and confusion takes its place. "I don't get it... You didn't show up and you wouldn't answer your phone... I thought you..." I have to battle to stay composed because it's one of my biggest fears: that she'll run and leave me. It's probably pathetic, but I can't help it. I don't need anyone else bailing out on my life, especially not Ella.

"I'm so sorry, Micha," she utters with wide eyes. "But I couldn't talk to you until I thought of the right thing to say."

"Talk to me about what?" My voice cracks with fear and I clear it.

"Talk to you about the wedding." She looks around like she's hunting for an escape route, but ultimately her eyes land back on me. "I talked to your mom the other day—she called me asking if I knew anything that you wanted for your birthday, and she also wanted to know if we were coming home for Christmas."

I raise my eyebrows in surprise. "Okay, that's nice I guess...but what does that have to do with skipping out on our wedding?"

She gives a disheartened sigh. "She asked if we'd set a date yet for the wedding yet. I didn't know you hadn't told her we were just going to get married here, without anyone."

My fingers stiffen on her cheek. "Did you tell her we were?"

"You know I'm a pro at lying."

I snort a laugh. "Not really, but we can pretend for now."

She shakes her head, her lips twitching to smile.

8

"Stop making jokes. I'm trying to be genuinely serious and honest right now."

"You...serious and honest?" I question with doubt, grinning amusedly at her. "Really?"

"I know. It's weird." She pauses, her chest nearly busting out of the top of her dress with each ragged breath. "I think..." She shifts her body, tucking her legs underneath her as she gets to her knees. "It's just that..." Her eyelashes flutter as she stares at the sunlight through the window. "I don't even know how to say this," she mutters.

I scoot forward on the bed, shoving the bulky material of her dress out of the way and getting close to her. "Pretty girl, whatever it is, you can say it. You can say anything to me. You know that." I just hope to God it's not what I'm thinking. That she's changed her mind. That she doesn't want to get married.

She tilts her head and our gazes meet. "I know, but it doesn't make it easier for me to say it. You know it's hard for me to say how I'm feeling."

I stroke the inside of her wrist with my thumb. "I know, but I'm always here for you." I'm trying to remain calm, but it's difficult. She's scaring the shit out of me, especially since I have no idea what the hell she's trying to say. I thought we had all this behind us. The day she put that ring on her finger was the happiest day

9

of my life and I thought I'd have many more happy moments with her to come, but now I'm worried I jumped to conclusions.

"And it's really hard for me to admit what I want sometimes," she continues, squeezing her eyes shut.

"I know it is," I say. "But like I said, you can tell me anything, even if it's bad."

Her eyelids lift up, her pupils shrinking as they hit the light. "I know and I think…I think we should just…" Her hand trembles in mine as her words rush out of her. "I think we should go home and have a normal wedding with our families." She presses her lips together and holds her breath.

I remain motionless, fighting to keep my laughter in, because I know it's going to piss her off, but eventually it gets to me and it slips out. "Oh my God." I nearly choke, wrapping my arm around my stomach. "I can't believe that's what this is all about."

"Micha." She pinches my chest through my shirt. "Stop laughing. I'm being serious."

"Oh, I know you are." I continue to laugh and the longer it goes on, the more irritated she gets, until finally she gathers her dress and scoots toward the edge of the bed to leave. I quickly circle my arms around her waist and draw her back down on the bed. She flops onto the mattress and I fold my body over hers, fighting through the bulky fabric to get close to her. As I press up against her, she tries to squirm out from under me, pressing her hands against my chest, but I pin her arms to the side of her head.

"It's not funny, Micha," she says hotly, but I can tell she's working really hard to stay angry with me. "I was trying to tell you how I feel and you laughed at me."

"I know I did and I'm sorry." I suppress my laughter the best I can. "But you're too fucking adorable for your own good."

She scowls. "I'm not adorable and you know it."

"When you tell me things like you want to have a wedding with our families and are nervous about it, you're fucking adorable." I dip my head down and gently kiss her cheek. "I love you and we can get married wherever, however, and whenever you want, just as long as we get married and you never *ever* stand me up again."

She pouts out her glossy bottom lip. "I'm sorry about that. I just panicked."

I nip at her bottom lip because it's too delicious to resist. "Next time, please just talk to me. Or at least send me a text." I kiss her again, then put a small amount of space between our bodies so I can look her in the eye. "A simple SOS or something."

"Deal," she says, but still seems anxious.

I hesitate. "Are you sure that's all that this is about?"

She swiftly nods. "Of course."

There's something in her green eyes I don't like, a familiar look that used to dwell there when we were growing up. Sadness, combined with fear and worry. I open my mouth to press her about it, but she arches her back and brings her mouth to mine. I distractedly kiss her, slipping my tongue deep into her mouth as all thoughts of abandonment and fear momentarily fade away.

I'm pretty sure it's the best ending to getting stood up on my wedding day. If only I could convince myself that there will be no more bumps in the road, but I worry about the look in her eyes and going home to get married. I'm worried about Ella. Even though things have been really good between her and her father and brother, sometimes during her phone conversations with them, one of them ends up bringing up the past and I know it upsets her. They're not trying to be hurtful. In fact, I have to give her father props for how much he's changed, although it still pisses me off that he ever let things get that bad. Let his daughter feel the blame for her mother's death to the point where she thought about taking her own life.

But he's been better about stuff and I remind myself that if Ella can have a nice version of her dad now, then she should have it. And she's been doing well, too, but she sometimes still struggles with depression and her fear of commitment. And I worry that it's the fear of commitment that is behind what just happened. That she's just stalling because she's not ready to marry me. And that maybe she really doesn't *want* to marry me.

Chapter Two

Ella

I'm trying to stay as calm as possible over the fact that I'm about to permanently seal my future, admit that I actually have a future, and give part of me to someone else. I've never been a fan of thinking far into the future, of thinking about what will happen when I get older, where I'll be. I avoid these kinds of thoughts mainly out of fear of what I'll see—who I'll become— and most of the time I just don't think I really deserve a future. But I don't want to be that girl who's so terrified of her past, who she is and the things she's done, that she can't move ahead in life. I don't want to be stuck motionless in a world crammed with self-loathing. I want to be strong, be someone who's worthy of love, who does things for the people they love.

I thought I'd arrived at that place, but then the box showed up in the mail yesterday, sitting on my doorstep like an omen, from some guy named Gary Flemmerton, a name I don't recognize, but what I did recognize was what was in the box—stuff that belonged to my mother. My thoughts got jumbled. I ended up doing something stupid. I stood Micha up at our wedding, not because I don't love him. I do. So, so much. But I'm confused. About the box. About what's inside it—the journal my mother wrote, her drawings, photos of her. It was her life, stuffed in a box, revealing things I never knew about her, like things that she drew or wrote.

I should be happy I got to discover some of her past. But for some reason discovering this just painfully brought up the past and it made me question my future. I started thinking about where I was going in life. Where will I be in five years? Will I be mentally healthy? Where will Micha and I be in our lives? Will we still live in San Diego? Will he still be playing music? Will I be working in an art gallery or selling my art? Will he still love me? Will we be happy? Will we have kids? The last thought is scary. I've never pictured myself as a mom and the only memories I have of my mom are the ones where I'm taking care of her. I don't want to do that to my own kids, make it so they have to take care of me.

On top of the panic over my future, I started feeling guilty that we were having a wedding without Micha's mom there. I could picture her getting upset, especially since she was the one who pushed us to get engaged. Micha would end up feeling bad, because that's what he does when someone feels hurt. Plus, there's this one other thing…something that I know sounds crazy, but I sort of want my mom nearby but the only way it's possible is to have the wedding in Star Grove where she's buried.

My mind was made up by the time Micha came back to the house but seeing him sort of unwound all the confused knots inside me. I'm still trying to sort through my thoughts, but I decide to take it one step at a time. After I get out of my dress and put on a pair of jeans and a T-shirt, I start packing up my stuff to go back home to Star Grove to have our wedding. I put the box with the journal into a large duffel bag to read later when I think I can handle it, along with my mother's sketchings and the wedding band I bought Micha.

"I think we should get married on Christmas," Micha announces as he exits the closet with a bag in his hand. He took his tux off and put it in the black bag so we can drop it off at the rental store. He now has on a pair of faded jeans, a black T-shirt, his black leather watch, and boots. As sexy as he looked in the tux, I prefer him this way because he looks like my

Micha. "It's the perfect day," he adds, setting the black bag down on the bed.

"Yeah, I guess," I say, pressing the fluffy wedding dress into the bag while trying to zip it up. It's actually Lila's dress. She lent it to me after we snuck into her parents' house and took it out of her closet. I also got to meet her mother during our little trip and the woman seems like a real bitch. I remembered the time Lila showed up at my house crying and it all started to make sense why she showed up that night at my house in Star Grove over a year ago in tears. But it's been a few days and she'll barely talk about it and I'm not the kind of person to force people to have heart-to-hearts. "But do we really want to share our anniversary day with another holiday?" I ask

"I like that you're thinking in advance." Micha drops his duffel bag on our bed and prods me with his elbow to move out of the way. Seconds later, he has the bag zipped up and the dress securely inside it. "But still, Christmas also marks the anniversary of when we got engaged." He looks down at the ring on my finger. "It'll be one year since I gave you that."

I lift my hand up in front of me and the black stone glimmers in the light, which highlights the scratches, marks, and dings. The beauty. The perfection. The meaning. "I like the idea of a Christmas wedding I guess, just as long as we don't have to have tacky Christmas decorations, like Santas and reindeer or something."

"You can have whatever kind of decorations that you want," he says as he drapes the black bag with the tux over his shoulder and then collects our bags. "Just as long as you'll marry me."

"You're too easy on me." I lower my hand to my side and smile, even though my nerves make my stomach roll. "But it's a deal. A Christmas-day wedding with no Christmas decorations."

He looks happy as he embraces and kisses me and then we go outside into the cool ocean air and put our bags next to Micha's 1969 Chevelle SS. He then runs back inside to get his keys because he left them on the counter. I stare at the inflatable Santa across the street waving at me, or maybe it's just the wind blowing him around. There's hardly a breeze here though, and nothing compares to the winter wonderland I'm willingly about to go back to. Star Grove. My hometown. The place where I broke apart and was put together again. The place that holds so many memories, both good and bad. I hope it's worth it. I hope nothing bad happens. I hope this trip will finally hold only good.

For some reason, I'm doubtful and the longer I stand there in the driveway, staring at the Santa, the more anxious I get. Finally Micha comes out of the house with Lila right behind him, heaving her suitcase down the steps and up the path. Micha kisses me when he reaches me, then unlocks the trunk and sets Lila's suitcase inside.

"Are you going to ask your dad to walk you down the aisle?" Lila asks cheerfully as I hand Micha my suitcase.

Micha looks at me curiously, waiting to hear my answer as he drops my bag into the trunk.

"There's not going to be an aisle." And I don't want my dad to walk me down it. Yeah, I don't mind him at the wedding, but I don't want him to be the person who guides me to the finish line when he wasn't that great for most of the journey.

Lila places her hands on her hips and narrows her blue eyes at me. "Oh, there's going to be an aisle. You'll see."

Micha laughs as he tosses Lila's suitcase into the trunk. "I think she means business, pretty girl."

I'm about to tell him to shut up when Ethan exits the house with his bag in his hand, squinting against the sunlight. "Are you two sure you don't want to just drive down to Vegas and elope?" he gripes as he approaches us, then chucks his duffel bag at Micha. "I really don't want to see my mom or dad or Star Grove— I've been enjoying my space from both."

"Baby, come on. Let them be. They deserve a beautiful wedding, not an elopement in a tacky fake church." Lila glides her hand up the front of his chest, stands on her tiptoes, and kisses his neck. Then she whispers something in his ear as she plays with his hair.

I'll admit they make a cute couple, especially now that Lila has this whole grunge thing going. Her blonde hair is chin length and streaked with black that matches Ethan's hair. She's wearing jeans and a tank top that aren't name brand like everything she used to wear when we were living together. Her style goes well with Ethan's laidback look: his plaid shirt and faded jeans and a pair of sneakers that he's probably owned since he was sixteen. And Lila's average height allows her to nestle her head against Ethan's chest comfortably. Looking at them with the sunlight and my house in the backdrop, I find myself wishing I had time to draw them.

After a lot of kissing and whispering in Ethan's ear, Lila convinces him to stop complaining and he begrudgingly agrees that Vegas is a ridiculous idea and that Micha and I should get married in Star Grove.

"A week is not a lot of time to prepare a wedding," Lila declares, pulling her sunglasses over her eyes. "Not a real one with decorations, flowers, dresses, tuxes, and guests. God, I wish we had more time to plan this."

"And I wish you wouldn't take any time to plan it," I say, and when she frowns I sigh. "Sorry, I'm just not into wedding stuff." I round the car to the passenger side of the Chevelle, trailing my finger across a few dings and chips in the black paint that were put there when Micha intentionally crashed it into the snow bank.

Micha opens the driver door and steps back so Ethan can climb into the backseat. "It doesn't matter what kind of wedding we have," he says, "just as long as Ella's there with me. In fact, we don't even need dresses and tuxes. We could even be naked and standing in my backyard and I'd be okay." He winks at me over the roof of the car. "As long as we're together, I'll be happy and being naked would just be an added bonus."

This makes Lila giggle as she ducks her head and hops into the backseat with Ethan. I push the seat back, get in the car, and shut the door, then pull the visor down to block the sunlight.

Micha adjusts the driver's seat before he closes the door and starts the engine. "So is everyone ready for this?" He looks around at the three of us, but when his eyes finally land on me I know he only really cares about my answer.

It takes me a second to answer and he notices my hesitation and his expression starts to fall. But even though my throat feels dry I manage to say, "Of course." My voice trembles a little.

"Okay then." Giving me a small but slightly forced smile, he backs down the driveway and drives down the highway, toward home where all of this started. Where Micha and I first met, first talked, first played, kissed, fooled around, danced, said I love you.

Where Micha and I began.

※

We drive down the dark, desolate highway for hours, the moon a bright orb against the black sky and the trees on the side of the road only outlines. Music is playing from the speakers and Ethan is snoring in the backseat with his head against the headrest while Lila leans against him. I have my sketchpad opened on my lap and a pencil in my hand.

I'm supposed to be working on my portfolio over Christmas break for graduation in May. I'm not even sure exactly what I'm going to do when I graduate with my associate degree, but it'll have something to do with art. Honestly, if I had my way, I'd spend all day with Micha, listening to him sing, while I draw things that mean something to me—things that move me. I wouldn't want to draw so I could sell my art. Yes, it would be an added bonus, but doing it as a job would take some of my passion for creating away.

Right now all the pages in my sketchbook are blank or have unfinished pictures on them because I wasn't feeling it and stopped. It's supposed to be full of pieces that mean something to me, that will make people experience emotion, tell a passionate story from the heart. I can't seem to find my angle and everything I start ends up feeling forced.

I wonder if my mom had this problem.

"So I'm trying to decide whether to tell my mom or not that we almost went through with a wedding without her," Micha says, slipping his fingers through mine, and the contact jerks me from my thoughts and I gasp, startling him and myself.

"Are you okay?" he asks. "You seem distracted."

"Yeah I'm fine…and I vote no." I set my pencil down and close my untouched sketchbook, since it's too dark to draw anyway, and put it down on the floor beside my feet. I rub my tired eyes, then slant my head to the side and watch the stars in the sky stream by in various illuminating colors, trying not to think about the journal tucked away in my bag in the trunk. My mom's journal and drawings. My mother who won't be at my wedding. I want to scream at myself because it shouldn't be such a big deal. She was hardly around when I was alive so what does it matter? Yet for some reason it does.

"What's the matter, pretty girl?" Micha glances at me and there's a tease in his tone. "Are you afraid she's going to get upset?" He releases my hand to sweep strands of his blond hair out of his aqua eyes that are so strikingly beautiful even the darkness can't conceal it.

"I'm never afraid," I assure him as he returns his fingers to mine, bringing me instantaneous warmth. "I'm just worried she's going to get upset and cry and then things are going to get awkward."

He chuckles softly, and then delicately kisses my knuckles, causing my heart to flutter. "So you're only worried about things getting awkward, huh?" The ring looped through his bottom lip grazes my skin as he moves his mouth away, and then he puts his hand to the shifter with our fingers still entwined. "There's nothing else bothering you at all? Like the fact that you're going to have to stand up in front of a group of people and tell them why you love me?"

I gape at him. "What are you talking about?"

"Our wedding vows," he says. "Did you forget?"

I look at the window to hide my guilty face. With the box arriving on my doorstep yesterday and the

24

panic of actually getting married, I'd completely forgotten about the vows. Micha had thought it'd be a great idea to write our own vows and I'd agreed because it was only going to be him and me, Lila, Ethan, and a minister. I knew there was no way I could write anything as poetic as Micha would. The boy is amazing with lyrics and letters and words in general. Myself, not so much, especially when it comes to writing about the heavy stuff like my feelings. I really suck at self-expression, unless it's through art. *I wonder if I could get away with just holding up a few drawings of him?*

"You did forget, didn't you?" Micha starts laughing again, looking so happy it hurts my heart, because I should be that happy. And I am, for the most part, but there's still stuff bothering me, like the journal, the vows, my future, what the hell I want to become of my life.

I smash my lips together and meet his gaze. "I might have let it slip my mind, but not because I don't love you."

"I know that."

"I know, but still..." I sigh. "I'm such an asshole."

He laughs even harder, one hand gripping the steering wheel as he merges into the other lane. "You're not an asshole." He skims his fingers across the bumps

25

of my knuckles with his thumb. "And we don't have to write our own vows if you don't want to. I'm perfectly content with just marrying you."

"You're so sappy sometimes," I tease, and then take a shaky breath. "But I want to do the vows." It's such a lie but I want to make him happy—he deserves to be happy. And this is something I can do to give that to him.

He cocks an eyebrow. "Are you sure?"

No. "Yeah, I'm absolutely sure." I sound kind of choked, but I don't think he notices. I feel bad, but at the same time I can't help how I feel. I'm never really sure about anything. I get anxious when it comes to huge decisions and that makes me hesitate every single time. If I had my way, it wouldn't be like that, but sometimes things are out of our control when it comes to who we are.

"Vows it is then." He smiles and it makes me sad. I want to be as happy as he is. I really do. But sometimes it seems like it's impossible, no matter how hard I try.

I fall asleep somewhere between the exit ramp and the bridge that stretches over the lake that's at the edge of Star Grove, the one I almost jumped off the night before I ran away to Vegas. By the time I open my eyes again, we're pulling up to Micha's old house, which is next door to mine. The sun is ascending from behind the mountains that surround our little town and snow blankets the lawns around us. It's freezing here, and the sidewalks and driveways are all glazed in ice. Silver, green, and red Christmas lights twinkle on some of the nearby houses, but most of the front yards in this neighborhood are decorated with broken-down cars, boxes, trash. There's a younger guy who I'm pretty sure is selling drugs on the street corner, and a guy yelling at his wife as she storms down the sidewalk in her pajamas.

"Welcome home," Micha mutters, and then yawns, stretching his lean arms above his head.

I cover my mouth as I yawn. "You should have let me drive a little. You seriously look tired."

"I am seriously tired," he says, silencing the engine. "And I plan on getting some sleep just as soon as you take a shower with me." He flashes me a grin and then pulls the keys out of the ignition. "That'll wear me out and I'll be able to fall right to sleep afterward."

"Dude, shut the fuck up," Ethan grumbles, making a disgusted face. His black hair is flat on one side where his head was against the window and he has his tattooed arms around Lila as she sleeps with her head on his chest.

"Hey, you can't give us crap," I tell Ethan, unbuckling my seat belt. "I'm officially scarred for life after yesterday."

"What happened yesterday?" Micha asks as he cracks open the door and cold air rushes into the car.

Ethan shoots me a dirty glare, but I ignore him. "I came home from work," I tell Micha, "and heard some very disturbing noises coming from the guest room."

"Nice," Micha says and then flinches when I punch him in the arm. "What? If it'll make you feel better we can make a whole bunch of noise in the shower and pay them back."

"Please don't," Ethan pleads grumpily as he stretches his free arm above his head. "I've heard enough from you two to last me a lifetime."

"Okay, this is getting really awkward," Lila mumbles with her eyes still shut. "Can we all just pretend that we haven't heard each other have sex...or phone sex?"

And that's my cue to get out of the car since she's referring to the time Micha and I had phone sex when I was still sharing an apartment with Lila while Micha was on the road. As I step out into the snow, Micha laughs and Ethan cracks a joke underneath his breath. Ignoring them, I slam the door and wind around to the back of the car, leaving my tracks in the snow.

Thankfully, I thought ahead and wore my lace-up

boots and a pair of jeans, otherwise I'd be freezing. I don't have a jacket on, though, and my hair's pulled up in a ponytail so my neck's exposed to the icy air. I wrap my arms around myself and wait for Micha to come open the trunk as I stare at my house next door.

I can tell my dad's been out and about because of the fresh tire tracks going up and down the driveway and the fact that his Firebird is parked near the back steps, the windows defrosted. Beside the car is the tree that Micha used to climb up almost every night to sleep with me. I used to hate the tree because I climbed up it the night my mom died, but now, looking at it, I can't help but smile because it was the thing that brought Micha to me many times.

"Baby, where's your jacket?" Micha asks as he struts around to the back of the car, slipping off his own jacket.

"I think it's in my suitcase." I force my attention away from my house and onto him as he hands me his jacket and I distractedly slip it on. He's so God damn gorgeous it's distracting. I wish I could just draw him all the time. He'd probably let me if I asked, telling me he belongs to me and I can do whatever I want with him.

I absentmindedly rub my thumb across the ring on my finger as I feel the reality of the thought. That we belong together. *Him and me. Forever.*

He looks down at my ring, then takes my hand and reaches out to sketch his finger around the diamond band twisted in knots that encase a black stone. "I'm still surprised how well you're handling this."

"What? Being engaged?" I shiver from the cold, or maybe it's from his touch.

A pucker forms at his brow as he glances down at the ring on my finger. "Over the fact that we're going to get married..." He looks over at my house. "Here, with everyone."

My muscles tense, but I joke to lighten the tension building inside me. "Give me a few days and we'll see if you still think I'm handling it well. You might not even want to marry me anymore."

"You know as well as I do that we're going to get married." His eyes darken with desire as his voice deepens. "Just like we both know that I'm going to fuck you when we take a shower in just a few minutes."

His voice sends tingles all over my body, a flurry of hot sparks. "I swear to God, you are the horniest person in the world."

"Nah, I'm just a guy who's completely attracted to his beautiful fiancée." He leans in to give me a kiss on the lips, before popping the trunk.

I grab my bag and slide the handle over my

shoulder. "You're always over complimenting me. You know that?"

He swings the duffel bag over his shoulder and looks like he's resisting an eye roll. "Don't worry, I'll stop when your head gets too big, but I doubt that'll ever happen." He picks up a large bag and chucks it over the roof of the car to Ethan, who catches it against his stomach with a grunt.

"Jesus, a little warning would be nice," Ethan says as he slides the handle of the bag over his arm.

Micha grabs Lila's suitcase and extends the handle, lowering the bag down to the snowy driveway. "You guys are staying here, right?" Micha calls out to Ethan, slamming the trunk shut.

Ethan shrugs, looking at Lila, who shrugs too. "I was planning on it." He drapes his arm around Lila's shoulder and she cuddles against his chest as they hike through the snow for the back door, leaving Micha and me to finish unloading the trunk by ourselves. "You know I like your place more than my own."

"Only because my mom lets us do whatever the hell we want," Micha points out.

"True," Ethan calls out.

We follow them to the side door of the house that's right in front of the garage where Micha used to work on his car all the time and I would hang out with him because it was the only place I felt at home.

"God, Lila, this thing is heavy," Micha remarks as he drags Lila's suitcase in the snow behind him. "What the hell did you pack?"

"Normal stuff," Lila says, looking offended.

Ethan opens the back door and steps into the kitchen. "She overpacks."

"Hey," Lila protests, bumping her elbow into Ethan's side as she steps into the house. "I'm a lot better than I used to be."

"True," Ethan agrees, following her in and letting the screen door bang shut.

"Is your mom home?" I ask as Micha lifts the suitcase up the steps.

He shrugs, opening the screen door. "Maybe." He pushes the suitcase into the kitchen while holding the door open with his elbow. "She might have had to work the morning shift, though, or she might be out with Thomas."

I hitch my finger through the handle of the bag. "But you told her, right? That we were coming?" I step inside the kitchen and into the warm air, stomping my boots on the mat just in front of the threshold. "And why we were coming?" I sound so nervous. Damn it. I need to chill out.

Micha shakes his head as he shuts the door. "I thought we could do it together."

My eyes skim the small kitchen I ate many meals in while I was growing up. If I hadn't, I probably would have starved. "Sounds good, I guess."

He pauses near the kitchen table. "Unless you're not okay with that."

"No, I'm okay with that," I tell him, attempting to push through my nerves. *You can do this. It's not that scary. You've been living together for six months. Hell, you've pretty much lived with him since you were four.* "We should do it together."

He nods, but his aqua eyes are still fixed on me, like he's trying to read my soul. I kind of wish he could so he would tell me what it says, because sometimes I'm not so sure.

After a few intense moments of staring at me, he gives me a smile and then grabs hold of my hand. He steers me around the narrow counter area and toward the hallway that leads to his bedroom. Lila and Ethan head to the other end of the house where there's a small guest bedroom Ethan used to crash in all the time while we were growing up.

Micha kicks his bedroom door open and I can't help but smile as vivid memories rush back to me: the room where we grew up, where we spent many nights together, where he proposed to me. They're beautiful memories and they remind me of why I'm going to marry him. I hold my breath for a moment as the thought slams straight into my chest again, like it did right before I was supposed to go to the wedding. My heart rate picks up as I glance at the window, thinking how easy it would be for me to run. I've done it once and I could do it again, but deep down in the bottom of my heart, buried below my anxiety, I know I don't want to. I suck a slow breath through my nose and exhale out my mouth. *Relax. You need to stop panicking.*

His bed isn't made and has probably been that way since the last time we were here a year ago. Drumsticks and a guitar are on the floor in front of the open closet and hanging on the wall are his favorite band posters, along with some of my drawings. Old clothes are piled on a chair near the window that looks out to the side yard of my house and to the leafless tree that extends to my bedroom window. His room still smells like him, too, as if the scent of his cologne is embedded in the carpet fibers. I've always loved the smell, a simple scent bringing me instant comfort even in the darkest times. I wonder if I just stand here and breathe it in over and over again if it can help me forget what's in the bag that's secured over my shoulder.

Micha chucks his bag on the unmade bed and turns to me, rubbing his hands together. "Ready for our shower?" he asks with a devilish grin.

I drop my bag onto the floor. "Yeah, just give me a second to get my clothes out. They're all buried beneath the wedding dress."

He crosses his arms and gives me an apprehensive look. "Are you sure you're okay? You've been acting really distracted and now you're acting like you don't want to be around me."

I plaster on the most generic smile. Deep down I know he probably can read right through my bullshit. "I'm perfectly fine." I place my hands on his shoulders and kiss his scruffy cheek. "But if you really want to know, I have some naughty little nighties in my bag that I don't want you to see, otherwise you'll make me try them on for you and they're for after we get married."

He cocks his head to the side, assessing me as he unzips his jacket. "Since when do you wear nighties?" He shucks off the jacket, balls it up, and tosses it on the dresser.

"Since Lila made me go into Victoria's Secret and buy them." Which isn't entirely a lie. That actually did happen, but I do feel like a jerk for not coming straight out and telling him about the journal and drawings.

"You know, I'm really starting to like Lila. She's such a good influence on you," he says cleverly and then kisses me deeply, slipping his tongue into my mouth before pulling away. "If you're not in the shower in five minutes, I'm coming back here naked to get you."

"Deal," I tell him and he heads out the door with a clean red T-shirt and jeans in his hand. As soon as the door shuts, I exhale loudly as I move my bag onto the bed. My fingers shake as I unzip it, and then I dig past the dress to the bottom of the bag and remove the box addressed to me, the return address from a Gary Flemmerton in Montana, but that's not who it's from, at least not according to the note inside the box, which was written by mother's mom—my grandma. And it makes no sense, because I've never talked to her before, yet she took it upon herself to write me a note and send me some stuff of my mother's. It's weird, yet at the same time it's got me thinking things I don't want to think, like maybe I could meet her, but then again, do I really want to let more people into my life?

The note's pretty simple and when I take it out of the box and read it again, I have the same reaction: confusion.

Ella, I know you don't know me and I'm so sorry about that. There were things that you probably don't understand, or maybe you do. Maybe Maralynn told you about me. Maybe she didn't. But regardless, I was going through the attic, cleaning it out, and found some of her old stuff. I thought that you'd like to have it. I was going to keep it myself, but it's just too painful. If you don't want it, you don't have to keep it. I just thought you might like it.

Then she signed her name in flawless cursive handwriting.

I'd only ever met my grandmother once and that was at my mother's funeral. We didn't say anything to each other and my father didn't talk to her. It makes no sense why she'd give me her phone number like I'd been the one avoiding her all these years. She could have come up to me at the funeral and said something, but instead she sat across from my dad, my brother, and me in the barely occupied church while the minister preached about life after death. I think she might have smiled at me once, but I wasn't completely sure at the time, nor did I care, because I was in a place where guilt was possessing my heart and mind. Plus, from what I knew about my grandmother, she wasn't a very nice person.

I'd heard my mom talk about her maybe only five

times and from what she told me, she was a horrible mother who treated her daughter like shit and who disowned my mom when she announced she was going to marry my dad. I guess my grandmother hated my dad and thought he wasn't good enough for her. That pretty much sums up everything I know and I've never talked to her to be my own judge. I'm not sure if I want to. The woman has been a shadow in my life. Then again pretty much everyone was a shadow in my life except for Micha. Micha has been my light in my dark life. I smile to myself, noting that I should put that in the vows.

My expression instantly sinks as I realize that eventually I'll have to write a page of heartfelt words and have to read them aloud, pour my heart and soul out to strangers. And when it's all done, Micha and I will be husband and wife. I'll have him forever and he'll have me. Just thinking about it, my pulse increases and my heart slams against my chest. It'll be just him and me forever, through thick and thin, through light and darkness. *Knock it off. You love him.*

I'm starting to freak out at the infinite future barreling at me, and I struggle to shake it off and concentrate on the box instead. I wedge my fingers through the opening in the top and remove the thing I'd been looking at when I'd been debating whether to go down to the cliff to get married. It's a black leather book, the cover faded, and inside is my mother's handwriting, stating her thoughts and feelings, her soul poured out across the many pages.

I open the journal as I sink down onto the bed. "For all of you who think you know me, you don't," I read aloud, running my fingers along the faded script. That's just the first page, and even reading it again puts goose bumps on my arms. It's as far as I've read and it seems like far enough, yet it doesn't. I've always wanted to get to know my mom better, the mom who didn't lie, didn't have panic attacks, the one who smiled, laughed, told jokes. Did she lie in these pages? Should I care so much? What's done is done. She's gone, and reading her journal isn't going to bring her back. Yet I do care.

"Ella." The sound of Micha's voice startles the living daylights out of me and I jump, slamming the journal shut.

He's standing in the doorway, completely naked just like he warned me he would be. Lean muscles carve his stomach and cursive letters tattoo the side of his rib cage in black ink, the first lyrics he ever wrote, which he swears he wrote for me: *I'll always be with you, inside and out. Through hard times and helpless ones, through love, through doubt.*

Setting the notebook down on my lap, I cover my mouth. "Oh my God. You're naked."

"Don't 'oh my God, you're naked' me." He enters the

room and his muscles ripple with his movements, causing heat to pool inside my stomach.

"What if Lila and Ethan saw you?" I ask, lowering my hand to my lap.

"Then they saw me," he replies, his eyes fastened on me as he shuts the door. "I told you I'd come in here naked and get you if you weren't in there in five." He rotates his wrist, pretending to check a watch that he's not wearing. "And it's been five."

I cross my legs because just seeing him like that makes me want to lie down on the bed and spread my legs open so he can slip inside me. "Well, I was coming."

"Oh, you will be in a few minutes." A grin flashes across his face but then it vanishes when he notices the box next to me and the journal on my lap. "What is that?"

I bite my lip guiltily. I haven't told him yet, because I know he'll worry about what it'll do to me. Still, I'm not going to lie to him now that he's asked. "It came in the mail yesterday. It's a box full of stuff... my mom's stuff."

His eyes widen and his lips part in shock. "What? Who's it from?"

I tap the top of the box with my finger. "Well, it says from a Gary Flemmerton, but the note inside is... well, it's from my grandmother... my mom's mom."

"Okay. Didn't your mom say she was mean?" he asks cautiously.

40

"Yeah, sort of." I smooth my hand over the journal with my chin tipped down. "But sometimes my mom lied about stuff."

He shifts his weight and sits down on the bed beside me. Then he hooks a finger under my chin and elevates it so I'm looking at him. "Do you want to talk about it?" he asks, looking at me with concern and making me feel at home, at peace, okay with everything, even the bad stuff.

"I can't just yet," I tell him and when he starts to frown, I add, "Not because I don't want to, but because I haven't even looked through all the stuff yet to know what I want to talk about."

"Do you want to go through it now? With me?" he asks with understanding.

"Not right now." I suck in a slow breath at the idea of reading my mom's thoughts, concerned about what they'll reveal, what they won't reveal. *Who was she? Was she like me once?* "But I will…I just need to process stuff one step at a time."

He nods, but still seems uneasy as he moves his finger away from my chin and puts his hand on his lap. "So who's this Gary guy? And why did he send it to you all of a sudden out of the blue? And why did he send it for your grandmother?"

"I have no idea, but here's the note." I pick up the

scrawled piece of paper from out of the box and hand it to him so he can read it for himself. After he skims over the note he looks even more perplexed as he sets it aside on the nightstand. "So she was just cleaning out the attic and thought, 'Hey, maybe I should send the granddaughter who I've never talked to a box of her mother's stuff? Or have this Gary guy send it for her'?"

"Maybe Gary's her boyfriend or something?" I lift my shoulders and shrug. "I have no idea because I've never talked to her before."

Micha glances at the note again, strands of his blond hair falling into his eyes as he shakes his head, worrying just like I knew he would. "This is really weird. I mean, how did they even get our address?"

"That's a good question." My mouth sinks to a frown as I look out the window at my small two-story house just next door, the one I grew up in, the one that is filled with painful, sad memories. There's snow falling and landing on the roof, which is missing half of the shingles. "Maybe from my dad."

"Yeah, but wouldn't he have said something to you about giving it to her?" he asks.

I aim a doubtful look at him because that doesn't sound like my dad at all. "Even though my dad's been better, he still gets weird about the past and my mom... Besides, I haven't talked to him in, like, a week." I swallow the massive lump lodged in my throat. "But I'll go ask him in a while."

Micha practically beams at me like he's so proud that I'm doing the mature thing and not running away from the problem. It makes me realize that I am and that I shouldn't be running away from marrying him, even though my initial instincts are screaming at me to bail out. It's been in me practically forever. Run when things get too deep, too emotional, too complex. I've run a lot, but I've been good lately and I want to keep doing well.

"Do you want me to go with you?" he asks with compassion in his eyes.

I nod, tucking loose strands of my hair behind my ears. "I do."

His smile broadens. "You remember those words very carefully. You're going to need to say them again soon."

"I do," I repeat with a playful grin as I bump my shoulder against his and it makes his smile stretch to his eyes. "I do. I do. I—" He swiftly slides forward and his lips silence me. At first it's a slow, warming kiss, but the longer it goes on the fierier and more passionate it gets. Suddenly his fingers are grabbing onto the bottom of my shirt and then he tugs the fabric up over my head. Chucking it aside, his lips crash back into mine again as he gets to his feet, pulling me with him. Then he picks me up in his arms and I can feel his hardness pressing up between my thighs as I secure my legs around his midsection. It feels so good and my body ignites with heat and eagerness and suffocates all the bad thoughts in my head. As he carries me across the hall, I don't even care if Lila or Ethan walks out and sees us. All I care about is being with him.

When he steps into the bathroom, music is playing from his iPod in the dock on the counter and the shower is on, the mirror fogged up from the heat and steam. The humidity in the air instantly clings to my skin as Micha bangs the door shut with his foot, sealing us in the sweltering room without breaking the kiss. He mutters an "I love you" over the lyrics of "The River" by Manchester Orchestra, and I utter the same thing back as he devours me with his hands and mouth. The feel of his lips, the soft sound of the lyrics, and the dampness of the steam absorbs into my skin and floods my veins with lust, need, hunger. They flood me with love.

God, I feel so loved sometimes I forget how to breathe.

Maybe I should put that in my vows, too.

Chapter Three

Micha

God, she's come so far, sometimes I can't even believe she's the same person I grew up with. The Ella I used to know would have run like hell if something like that journal showed up on the doorstep, but this Ella is handling it beautifully. Even though I love her no matter what—runner, Stepford wife, or crazy and impulsive—my heart grows more in love with her with each day, for the person she was, is, and the people we are together as a couple. Soon to be husband and wife. I just pray to God we get to that place. Deep down I know we will; it's just that I'll feel so much better once she says "I do."

My hands travel all over her body, feeling the flawlessness of her skin, her smooth stomach, her perfect neck, and then I taste her lips as my tongue explores every inch of her mouth. She tastes fucking amazing, like cherry lip gloss and peppermint.

I pull away with one of my hands pressed to her lower back, and the other gripping her thigh that's hitched around my hip. "What do you taste like?" I ask as her eyelids flutter open.

"Huh...what..." She breathes dazedly, like she barely has any idea of where we are. "Gum...I think...why?"

"You taste like cherries and mint." I lick her lips with my tongue and then set her down on the floor. "It tastes good."

She unlaces her boots and kicks them off as I unbutton her jeans and jerk them down her long legs. She's wearing a pair of black lacy panties that cover half of her sexy ass and I run my finger along the little pink bow that's sewn on the front of them. "I haven't seen these before," I say.

"I told you," she says, breathless. "Lila made me buy naughty lingerie." She tugs the elastic out of her hair and her auburn locks slip out of the ponytail and fall to her shoulders in waves, damp with the moisture from the shower.

I reach behind her to unhook her bra and the straps immediately fall off her shoulders. Her breasts spring free, her nipples perking as they hit the air. "God, you're beautiful." I leisurely take in the sight of her long legs and amazing body.

She shakes her head, like she always does whenever I give her a compliment, but before she can protest, I bend down and suck one of her nipples into my mouth, silencing her.

Her neck arches and her head falls back as she knots her fingers through my hair, moaning. "Micha..." She drifts off as I massage her nipple with my tongue while my hands wander to her panties. Hitching a finger in the top, I tug them down and she meets me halfway, kicking them off when they reach her knees. I return my mouth to her nipple as I slip my fingers up her bare thigh, not stopping until I'm inside her.

"Oh God..." Her knees start to buckle, her back pressing against the edge of the counter. I move my fingers inside her as my mouth makes a path back and forth between her breasts, sucking her nipples into my mouth and tracing circles with my tongue. Her hand glides up my back, gently scratching lines on my skin, and when she reaches my shoulders, she grips tightly, holding on to me.

I continue to kiss her breasts and feel the inside of her with my fingers as she veers closer to the edge, but eventually I crave more. Drawing my mouth away from her nipple and pulling my fingers out of her, I trail kisses down her stomach and her hands fall from my shoulders as I get down on my knees. She gasps as I bury my face between her thighs and slip my tongue inside her, my hands on her hips, gripping at her flesh. I taste her until it drives us both mad and her body tightens and her back arcs. She gasps in bliss as she clutches the counter for support.

By the time she returns to reality, I'm rock hard and desperate to be deep inside her. A groan escapes my mouth as I stand up, licking my lips before I seal my mouth to hers. Then I blindly steer us toward the shower, fumbling around until I find the curtain and pull it back. I break the kiss only to get us in the shower, and then once we're under the showerhead, I go straight back to kissing her. Warm water rivers down our bodies, our skin soaked as our hands explore each other. We kiss until we can't breathe, until my heart is slamming inside my chest, until she's trembling uncontrollably, then I delve my fingers into her hips, pick her up, and with one hard thrust I slip deep inside her.

She sucks in a breath, her arms looping around my neck and her legs wrapping around my waist, so she's fully opened up to me. I pull slightly out of her and then sink into her again with my hand braced against the shower wall. With each rock of my hips, she clutches onto me tighter, her back bowing, her breasts pressing against my chest.

"I love you," she whispers against my lips, shutting her eyes, our bodies moving rhythmically.

"I love you, too," I say, holding onto her as we both come apart together.

Chapter Four

Ella

I've opened a Pandora's box and there's no turning back. After I got out of the shower, I started working on my portfolio some more, but I became really frustrated when I couldn't get the creative juices flowing, so I decided to read my mom's journal and now I can't seem to stop. We've been at Micha's house for only a day and I'm halfway through the damn thing, the house too empty and quiet to distract me from reading every last word my mother wrote.

Micha found out that this morning his mom was with Thomas and now she's working the night shift at the diner. She won't be home until morning and Micha and I decided we'll talk to her when she gets home, to announce the news. Micha and Ethan took off a couple of hours ago to the grocery store to restock the cupboards that weren't full enough to feed their "hungry man bellies." Their words not mine. And Lila's taking a shower.

I'm sitting at the kitchen table, wearing one of Micha's shirts and a pair of jeans. It's chilly due to the fact that Micha's mom always leaves the heat low to save money. It's part of Star Grove life though; half the town is in poverty because a plant shut down a long time ago. We did it at my house, too, sometimes leaving the heat off intentionally and sometimes unintentionally when I forgot to pay the bill or there wasn't enough money to pay it.

I have a cup of coffee in front of me, along with the journal. The first ten pages are fairly normal, talking about prom and her love for art, although her words are a little mopey. I never even knew she liked to draw but from the few drawings in the box, it looked like she had talent. It's kind of nice to read about her like that, but then things start to get dark and the warm, fuzzy feelings I was having getting to know that artistic side of my mom shift into chills, especially when I get to the part about my dad. At first she seemed excited to be dating him. Like, really excited, to the point where she almost seemed high. But then the excitement went quickly downhill, reminding me of all those times when she seemed okay and then suddenly she wasn't.

*I'm not sure who I am anymore. I feel like I'm
lost all the time. When I look in the mirror, the
person I see isn't the person I used to be. Instead
of eyes, I see two empty holes. Instead of a mouth,
I see lips sewn together. I don't know what's happening to me. What changed in me. What made
me feel like my skin is molting off as I turn into
a different person who can't even walk anymore
without a lot of effort. If I had my way, I'd sit in
bed forever.*

Until I died.

*But I can't do that now. I have a responsi-
bility. A child growing in my belly and a man
who will be my husband in just a few weeks.
It's terrifying and not the life I think I want. But
there's nowhere else to go and really any other
alternative is just as bleak as the one before me.
Any future is, and sometimes just having one is
frightening.*

The entry was written when she was eighteen, right
before she married my dad. She was pregnant with
my older brother, Dean, something I didn't know. Her
thoughts are terrifying, especially since I've recently
been contemplating my future and where kids fit into
the mix. But I don't get it. My dad once told me that

she used to be happy in the beginning, but if that's the case, then when was he talking about? When was the beginning? Because in the journal entry she'd known him for only six months and she already seemed to be falling into the dark hole of despair that I'm very familiar with, no matter what I do or try to change about my life. In the end, I have depression. It'll always be with me—with Micha and me. I've known this for a while and yet I'm still going forward with him, always crossing my fingers he never regrets it.

But what if he does?

I take out a drawing that's folded up in the back of the journal along with a photo of my mom on a bed with her chin on her knees and her hair falling into her green eyes that look exactly like mine. She's smiling, but there's something off about the snapshot, like she's forcing herself to look happy, or maybe that's just what she looked like when she was happy. It's hard to tell sometimes and most of the time when I knew her, she just looked lost. She doesn't look lost here, but she doesn't look like she's someone who's got everything figured out. I wonder if that's what I look like?

The drawing is of this vase with a single rose inside it and the petals are cracked and wilting, piling up around the bottom. It hurts my heart looking at it, because as an artist, I can guess what place her thoughts were at when she drew it because I've been in that place.

"Oh my God, Ella, you did not ball up your wedding dress and shove it in a duffel bag." Lila huffs as she stomps into the kitchen with an overflowing armful of fabric and a rolled-up magazine. She's wearing a holey pair of jeans and a plain pink T-shirt, her blonde and black hair damp. "Seriously, why would you do that?"

"I'm sorry." I quickly shut the journal, regretting having opened it in the first place. Maybe I wasn't ready to read it. Maybe I should just let the past go. I'd been doing so well and I've even been off my medication. *But I want to understand her.* "I didn't even think about it when I stuffed it in there."

Lila lets the bottom of the dress go, but holds onto the top, examining the fabric. "It's all wrinkled now." She scrunches her nose at the front of the dress as she fiddles with one of the black roses on it. "We're going to, like, have to hang it up in the bathroom and steam the wrinkles out."

"The bathroom should be all steamed up from your shower." I bring the brim of the mug to my mouth. "So you could hang it up now."

"Yeah, it was already steamed up from your shower." She rolls her eyes and then laughs off her irritation. "You two and showers...I don't get it."

"Well, you really should," I say, unable to restrain a smile as thoughts of Micha and his hands and tongue overtake me. The dark thoughts the journal instilled in my head evaporate like the steam coming from the mug, although I'm fairly sure they'll be back if I continue to read it. "You're really missing out."

She drapes the dress on the back of the chair and sits down across the table from me. "Then maybe I'll have to try it sometime with Ethan."

Quiet settles between us as she opens up the magazine she was carrying, and I realize it's a wedding magazine. We've been friends for almost two and a half years now and it still feels like we hardly know each other sometimes. Perhaps it's because of my lack of being able to talk deeply about things or because it seems like we both like to carry our secrets.

"So you and Ethan," I start, setting the mug down on the table. "How's that going?"

She shrugs, restraining a grin as she flips a page of the magazine. "Good, I guess."

"Do you, like, love him?" I make a mocking swoon face. I never had any girlfriends when I was growing up. Instead I was mostly surrounded by Micha and his friends or my brother and his friends, so sometimes acting girly is weird.

Lila lowers her hand onto the table and then crosses her arms. "I think I do."

"Think?" I ask. "Or know? Because I heard you both know."

Her brows furrow. "Did Ethan tell Micha that we said I love you?"

I nod and take another sip of my coffee. "They do that sometimes, you know. Tell each other their secrets like a couple of girls."

"Well, they are friends," she says. "They should tell each other stuff."

I nod and wonder if I should tell her about my fear of writing and saying my vows, since I can't discuss it with Micha. She could help me figure stuff out. Maybe. Although I don't think she could help me with the fear of getting married, which might be behind the reason why I can't write my vows.

Before I can say anything, though, she suddenly rises from her chair with a big grin on her face. "I almost forgot. I got you a present."

"Why?" My expression falls. No one's ever given me presents except Micha and I'm not really a fan of getting them.

"For your wedding, duh." She rolls her eyes like I'm being absurd and then heads back to the guest room.

A few minutes later, she returns with a big pink gift bag in her hand. "Here you go, bride-to-be," she singsongs and then hands it to me. "I was going to give it to you yesterday, but...well, you know. Things happened."

"Yeah, I know." I set the bag down on the table. "That really wasn't about my panicking about getting married. I promise."

She plops down in the chair and props her elbow on the table. "Then what was it about?"

"Stuff." I'm hesitant, and when she presses me with a look, I decide to let her in on my life just a little, especially since I recently learned her parents haven't always been that great to her either. "I'm just worried about stuff in the future."

She slumps back in the chair. "Well, that's normal, Ella. Everyone worries about their future, especially when they're about to get married and are starting a future with someone else."

"Yeah, I guess you're right. I should probably just try to relax." But even when I say it, it doesn't seem possible. Relax. Sure, it's easy when I'm in Micha's arms or he's inside me and everything else around me—life—feels nonexistent. But alone without his comfort I'm hyperaware of the things that lie inside me, the dark things that could overwhelm me with sadness at any moment—I could lose myself at any moment.

We sit quietly as fluffy snowflakes melt against the windows and leave thin trails of water on the glass.

Eventually Lila sits up and attempts to look happier. "Okay, enough with the sad. You need to open my present."

I make a wary face at the gift bag and then open it up. There's decorative paper inside and a box sealed with a bow. I set it down on the table, then untie the bow and lift the lid. The first thing I come across is a blue garter trimmed with white lace. I take it out and put it around my wrist.

"You know that doesn't go there, right?" Lila teases, sitting up in the chair. "And it's your something blue."

"How very traditional of you," I say playfully and Lila smiles as I move onto the next item, a silver bracelet with a heart charm on it.

"And that's your something borrowed," she informs me. "You have to give it back to me when the wedding's over."

"It's pretty," I tell her, even though it's not really my style. But I appreciate it—her making the effort. "But I thought the dress was my something borrowed?"

She shoves the magazine aside and crosses her arms on the table. "Nah, you can keep the dress and consider it your something old. It doesn't hold anything but painful memories for me anyway."

"Are you sure?" I ask.

"I'm positive," she assures me and then gestures at the box. "Take the next thing out. It can be your something new."

I direct my attention back to the box and remove a much smaller box inside it. Inside, there's some red, lacy fabric, which I take out and hold up. "Jesus, this is skanky," I say wiggling my fingers through what look like nipple holes.

She giggles. "Skanky but fun."

I sigh, stick my hand into the box, and pull out a sequined thong. "Is this the bottom part or something?"

"It's whatever you want, I guess," she says with humor in her voice. "It could even be for Micha."

I snort a laugh and drop the thong onto the lacy fabric. "This is like a sex kit, isn't it?"

She shrugs, examining her nails. "I went into this really questionable store with sex toys and lingerie and told the clerk to pick out the best newlywed gifts.",

I slip the garter off my wrist and add it to the pile with the thong. "So you have no idea what's in here?"

"Not a clue except for the garter and the bracelet—I added those myself. But I'm dying to find out."

"Okay, now I'm really intrigued." I reach in and remove the next item, a feather duster with a really long handle. "What is this for?" I run my fingers along the feathers and then shiver. "It tickles."

She giggles, twirling a strand of her short hair around her finger. "I think that's the point," she says and I extend my arm across the table and tickle her face with it. "Hey, what the hell?" She laughs as I pull it away. "That's not for me and I'm pretty sure you're not supposed to tickle faces with it."

"It could be for you. You and Ethan could totally use it." I set the feather duster on top of the pile and reach for the last item, which is in another box, a long narrow one.

"You really want to go down that road?" she questions. "The one where we talk about our sex lives?"

I shrug as I open the top of the smaller white box, and then tip it to the side so batteries fall out. "You used to tell me all the time about the guys you hooked up with." I pick up the batteries, scrunching my forehead.

Her expression plummets and she abruptly becomes uncomfortable. "Yeah, but I'm not hooking up with some guy. I'm hooking up with Ethan and in the past you two didn't always seem like the best of friends." She snatches the batteries from me with inquisitiveness in her expression and this weird look crosses her face.

"Yeah, we've been better lately though, and besides, regardless if Ethan and I are getting along, you can talk about stuff with me," I tell her as I stick my hand into the narrow box. "I just don't want to hear all the details…" I trail off as I take out the item inside it. "What in the love of God, Lila? I mean, I knew this was a sex kit, but really?"

Lila's face turns bright red as she busts up laughing, her shoulders hunching forward. "I was sort of wondering if that was what was in there when the batteries fell out."

I hold up a pink vibrator with this weird front part attached to it, biting my lip not to laugh. But Lila continues to laugh as she extends her arm across the table and takes the vibrator out of my hand. Then she pops the batteries inside the bottom, twists a nob, and it starts to hum. Laughter escapes both our lips as she drops it on the table and it begins to shake.

"Imagine how good it will feel," she says, tears slipping through her eyes, her whole body trembling with laughter.

Still laughing, I ask, "Was the cashier who put this all together a guy or a girl?"

"A guy," she says, poking the vibrator with her finger to steer it away from falling off the table. "A total creeper appar…" she drifts off as the back door swings open. Snowflakes flurry in as Micha and Ethan come strolling inside, tracking snow and carrying a few plastic bags of groceries.

Micha takes one look at the vibrator, the pile of lacy and sequined fabric, and the feather duster and the bags immediately fall from his hands as he explodes with laughter. "What the hell did we miss?" He grips onto the countertop for support as his knees buckle.

Ethan stands by the backdoor, looking lost, like he can't quite figure out what the hell we were doing.

Lila overlaps her fingers as she leans back in the chair. "We were playing a game."

"What kind of a game?" Ethan wonders and the confusion is replaced by a wicked look. "See who could stick it farther up their——"

Lila cuts him off as she picks up the vibrator and chucks it across the room. It zips past his head and hits the door, still humming. "Do not finish that sentence, Ethan Gregory."

We all settle briefly into an awkward silence and then everyone spurts out in laughter. We continue to laugh until Micha scoops the vibrator up and turns it off. The humming stops and he puts it down on the table in front of me, winking at me as he backs up to where he dropped his groceries.

"So we were thinking of having a party," he announces as he piles the bags onto the kitchen counter.

I make a face as I put the vibrator, lingerie, and feather duster into the bag. "Really?"

He picks up a box of cereal out of the bag. "It'll be like a bachelorette slash bachelor party."

"Aren't we supposed to have those separately?" I ask, pushing the bag aside.

"And with strippers," Lila adds, and Ethan gives her a strange look as he slips off his jacket and hangs it up by the back door.

"Yeah, we could do that but I'd rather have a party with you," Micha says. "And you can always strip for me later when it's over. That's much better in my opinion."

"TMI," Ethan says with a frustrated sigh as he sets the bags he was carrying on the counter. Micha rolls his eyes at him and then turns to me. "So are you down?"

"For a party?" I ask. "I guess."

"You guess?" he questions, as he puts the cereal box into the cupboard. "We don't have to if you don't want to."

"It's fine. A party sounds fine." I get up from the chair and walk across the kitchen to him. I cross paths with Ethan as he heads for Lila. He whispers something in her ear and then the two of them wander off toward the guest room, Ethan muttering that they'll be back in a few.

I start helping Micha unpack the groceries, putting cans of food into the cupboard. "Who are you planning on inviting to this party of yours?" I ask.

He shrugs as he opens the fridge to put a gallon of milk away. "Just the people we used to hang out with. The ones still living around here anyway."

I close the cupboard and lean against the counter. "Which is probably pretty much everyone," I mumble and then internally sigh. "Are you going to play at this party?"

He kicks the fridge door shut and goes back over to the bags. "Do you want me to play at this party?"

I stare down at the floor. "If you want to."

He pauses and I continue to stare at the linoleum floor until his boots appear in my line of vision, and then I angle my chin back to meet his eyes. "What?" I ask as he aims a suspicious look at me.

"What do you mean, what?" He positions himself in front of me, his jacket still speckled with wet spots from the falling snow outside. "This is bothering you and I want to know why."

"It's not bothering me," I start to protest but he targets me with a warning look. "It's just that this will be the first party we've ever been at as a couple."

"And?"

"And from my knowledge, a lot of the people who came to these parties…the female ones…" I search for the right words that won't make me sound like a jealous asshole, but there aren't any so I decide to just be blunt. "You fucked."

He winces, but then quickly composes himself. "I know, but that's in the past. What matters is that I'll be fucking *you* at the end of the night, over and over again. In fact, I'll be fucking you every night for the rest of your life." He gives me a flirty smile and I swat his chest with my hand.

"What?" he says innocently, trapping my hand against his chest. "Would you rather me say 'make love'?" He brushes his thumb across the ring on my finger. "Because we can do that, too." With one swift movement, he slides his palm down my side, grips my hip, and spins me around. Pushing down on my lower back, he presses up against me as I grip onto the counter for support.

"It's really up to you." His breath caresses my ear before he draws his mouth away to nibble on my earlobe.

I shudder and his chest collides against my back as he laughs. "Of course if we make love then the vibrator isn't going to be much use," he says.

"It's a gift from Lila."

"It looks fun." His voice comes out gravelly.

"Fun for me or for you?" I joke.

His hair tickles the back of my neck as he leans his head against me, sucking in a slow breath. "Keep it up, pretty girl, and you're going to get it."

"Maybe that's what I'm aiming for." I bite my lip in anticipation, waiting for him to react.

He misses a beat and I feel him shift his hips. "I swear to God, you're going to be the death of me." His lips touch the back of my neck, feather soft, and then he rubs his hips against me before stepping away, and I turn around and we return to putting the groceries away.

I notice him glance at the closed journal on the table a couple of times, but he doesn't say anything about it. Eventually, I decided to answer the question I know he wants to ask but isn't going to because he knows it's better for me to bring it up.

"I read some of it," I admit as I stand on my tiptoes to put a can of beans on the top shelf.

"And how was it?" he casually asks as he rummages through the last bag of food.

I hop up onto the counter, letting my legs dangle over the side. "Intense."

"How so?"

I shrug. "Her thoughts were just dark and I found out that she was pregnant with Dean when she decided to marry my dad."

He positions himself in front of me and urges my legs open so he can step in between them. "Really?"

I nod, pressing my knees against his side. "And she was scared."

"Of being a mom?" His hands clamp down on my thighs.

"And having a future." Tears sting at my eyes. The words are striking a nerve. A painful, aching nerve, buried deep inside my heart. I massage my hand over my chest, trying to get the crushing pain out.

Sensing my panic, Micha quickly wraps his arms around me. The second I'm in his arms, I feel better, lighter. He hugs me as I breathe. *Breathe. Breathe. Breathe.* I bury my face in his chest and he supports my weight like he always does. *Always.*

"Are you really sure you want this for the rest of your life?" I mutter against his chest.

"More than anything, Ella May." He kisses the top of my head. "I've known that since the day we met."

The tears subside as I look up at him. "You've known you wanted the crazy girl next door to be your wife since you were four?"

He nods, holding my gaze. "Maybe not as a wife,

but I knew from the moment I saw you that I wanted you in my life forever."

Tears make their way back up, this time not out of panic but from the overwhelming abundance of emotions I feel for him. God damn it, it's so intense. Too intense. Feelings built over years and years of history, starting with the moment we first met.

"You were always there for me," I say. "No matter how much of a pain in the ass I was."

He smiles. "And even though you won't ever admit it, you were there for me, too, every time I needed you."

I want to disagree with him, but I don't because it'd ruin the moment. "Just you and me against the world," I whisper as tears drip from my eyes and down my cheeks.

He fixes a finger underneath my chin, slants my head back, and leans in to kiss me. "Always and forever."

Chapter Five

Micha

Four years old . . .

I love spending time with my dad, especially when he works on cars 'cause it's the only time when he really talks to me and does stuff with me. He's working on the Challenger while I play with my toy car, driving it really fast back and forth across the Challenger's bumper.

"Micha, can you hand me that wrench?" my dad says with his head tucked underneath the hood. It's a really old car that he's working on fixing up, but it seems like it's taking him forever. I don't know why he just doesn't drive it the way it is now. I think it looks pretty fun and all the sides are different colors.

I jump off the bumper and dig around in his toolbox near the back end until I find the wrench and then I walk to the front and hand it to my dad.

"Thanks," he mutters and goes back to working on the engine.

I get a juice box out of the cooler, lean against the fender, and stare at the next-door neighbors' house. It looks a lot like mine, but there is a lot of trash and car parts are everywhere and it looks like nobody ever cleans up.

I'm about to head back to the trunk when the door swings open and the girl who lives next door steps outside. She looks like she's going to cry, but she looks like that almost every time I see her. She's got hair that's the same color as our red mailbox and every time I talk to her, her eyes remind me of leaves. Her name is Ella and she always has tears in her eyes. I'm not sure if it's because her mom is yelling at her all the time or because they make her take out the trash every day. Whatever it is, she always looks like she's gonna burst into tears. I asked my dad once why the neighbors were always yelling and he said it's because they are a messed-up family.

I grab another juice box out of the cooler and wave to her as I step out of the garage. She doesn't wave back, but she's usually shy at first, like she thinks I'm the boogeyman or something. With her head tucked down, she wipes the tears out of her eyes and walks down the steps. She doesn't have any shoes on and the cement has to be hot under her feet.

"Hey, Ella," I say, walking up to the fence between our houses.

She stands at the corner of her house with her arms crossed, staring at the ground. She barely talks, and half the time, even when she's talking, she looks down at her feet or the ground or at the trees.

I hear her mother yelling in the house, telling Ella she needs to come clean up the dishes. My mom says I'm too young to help with the dishes, even though my dad says I should be helping out more.

Ella keeps wiping her eyes with her hand as her mom yells from inside the house and I wonder if she's hiding from her mom. Finally, the yelling stops and Ella dares to look at me.

I hold up one of the juice boxes, offering it to her, hoping she'll come over to my house for once. "Do you want one?"

She looks at me for a really long time and then she slowly walks toward me. She pauses at the grass, looking like she's scared to come closer, so I reach my arm over the fence. She stares at the juice box, then runs up and takes it.

"Thank you, Micha," she says quietly, stepping back as she pokes the straw into the juice box.

"You're welcome," I tell her, as she starts slurping on the straw.

I feel bad for her. I don't think her parents take care of her because she always seems really thirsty and hungry every time I offer her a snack. I've tried to get her to come over and play a few times, but she always says she can't.

"Micha, get in here," my dad calls out from the garage and he sounds really mad. "I need your help."

Ella instantly steps back, her eyes widening. "Bye, Micha."

"You should come over," I call out and hold my toy car through the hole in the fence. "This is my favorite one, but I'll let you play with it."

She eyes the car and then glances back at her house. "I think my mom might get mad at me if I do."

"You can just come over for a little bit," I suggest. "Then when your mom comes out looking for you, you can climb back over the fence. Besides it's really fun watching my dad work on the car."

She glances back and forth between the house and the car in my hand and finally she hurries back toward her house. I think she's going back inside, but instead she grabs a plastic box that looks like the thing I keep all of my toy cars in. She drags it over to the fence and steps up on it. She takes a gulp of her juice box and then she hands it to me and I step back as she climbs over the fence. She falls down on her knees as she lands and cuts one of her knees a little.

"Are you okay?" I ask her.

She nods, looking like it doesn't hurt at all as she wipes the dirt off and stands back up. She grabs the juice box and toy car from me and I smile as I walk back toward the garage with her, happy I finally got her to climb over the fence.

Ella

Six years old . . .

I like my next door neighbor Micha a lot. At first he was kind of scary because he was so nice and no one's ever been that nice to me before. But now he's not too scary. He always shares his juice and cookies with me at school and when Davey Straford pulled my hair and told me I was icky because I had holes in my clothes, Micha shoved him down and told him he smelled like rotten eggs.

The teacher got mad at him and then his dad got mad at him when we got home from school. He couldn't play with me for three days 'cause his mom and dad said he was grounded, but it's been three days and now I can go over again.

It's a really hot day, so I get two Popsicles out of the freezer before I head over. My shoes have got holes in the bottom of them again so I don't even bother putting them on. My mom yells at me to take out the trash as I walk out so I have to go back and haul it out of the trash can. She's always yelling at me to take out the trash and do the dishes. It makes me sad sometimes because I get tired, but my dad says she's sick and my brother and I have to be nice to her and help her out because he has to go out at night to "clear his head and take a break."

The garbage bag's really heavy and leaves this gross slimy stuff on the kitchen floor as I drag it out, slide it off the steps, and toss it into the bigger trash can. I put the lid on and skip down the sidewalk and then climb over the fence.

The sprinklers are on and the grass is all wet and kind of muddy, but I splash in it anyway, getting the bottom of my jeans wet, and some mud gets stuck in my toes. I skip up the sidewalk, making footprints on the cement all the way to the side door of Micha's house.

I'm about to knock on the door when I hear someone crying from inside the garage. The door is open and Micha's dad's Challenger isn't inside and it's always parked in there, so it's weird. Micha's dad is always working on it and getting mad at it. When I get inside the garage, I find Micha sitting where the car used to be parked, with his back turned to me. It sounds like he's the one crying, which makes no sense. Usually I'm the one crying and Micha is the one smiling.

"Micha," I say and the crying stops.

"I can't play today, Ella," he says quietly, and it looks like he's trying to wipe tears away.

I walk around in front of him, but he won't look up at me, so I sit down on the floor. He tucks his arms onto his lap and I can only see the top of his head, because he's looking down at the ground.

"Micha, what happened?" I ask, the Popsicles cold in my hand.

He shakes his head and then his shoulders begin to shake as he starts crying again. "My dad took the car and left."

"I'm sure he'll be back soon," I tell him, not understanding why that's making him cry. My dad leaves in his car all the time.

He shakes his head and looks up at me. Micha's eyes are this really pretty blue color that I saw on these beads once that I used to make a bracelet at school. His eyes are really wide and shiny right now like the beads and he looks so sad. It kinda makes me feel like crying, too.

"No, he's not coming back," he tells me and tears roll down his cheeks and fall onto the ground. "Ever. My mom said he ran away and he's never coming home."

I don't know what to say to him. My dad ran away once, too, at least that's what my mom told me, but then he came home that night and my mom said it must have been because he couldn't find anywhere else to go. But sometimes she tells stories that I don't think are true.

I scoot closer to Micha, not sure what to say to him, so instead I hold out a Popsicle. He keeps crying as he looks at it and then he finally takes it from my hand. He peels the wrapper off and I peel mine off and then I sit there with him while he cries because it always makes me feel better when he sits with me when I'm upset. Eventually his tears stop, long after the Popsicles are melted in our bellies and Micha finally gets up and wipes his eyes with the back of his hand. I get to my feet, too, and I search for something to say.

"Do you want to do something?" I ask.

He glances at me, still sad, but then he nods. "Yeah, what do you want to do?"

I smile and take his hand. "Whatever you want to do," I say. He's usually doing stuff for me, but today it should be about making *him* happy.

He considers something and then there's the slightest sparkle in his eyes. "How about hide-and-go-seek?"

I nod and then we play until the sun goes down, turning a sad day into a decent one because we're together.

Chapter Six

Micha

Later that day, I rap my hand on the doorway as I walk into my bedroom. Ella is lying on the bed on her stomach with the journal opened in front of her. I really wish she'd stop reading that thing. As much as I know it's good for her to have something that belonged to her mom, I can see in her eyes that whatever's in there is bringing her down. She hasn't been on her medication for a while and hasn't talked to a therapist in a few months, at least that I know of. She's been doing fine and I want her to stay that way, but I also don't want to be the asshole who tells her to quit reading her dead mother's journal.

So I keep my mouth shut and instead check her out. She's beautiful, her auburn hair pinned behind her head, wavy curls framing her face, and she's wearing a black-and-red dress that hugs her body and black stilet-tos on her feet.

"God, you're so fucking hot," I say, adjusting myself as the urge to slam the door and take her from behind tries to overpower me. But people have started to arrive at my house for the party, so I control myself.

Ethan is letting everyone in but he wasn't too happy about the party to begin with. Although I have no idea why because he used to enjoy parties back when we were younger. It was our thing and we probably threw more at my house then we actually went out to, since my mother never cared just as long as we cleaned up afterward. I had to laugh at Ethan when we were driving and chatting about what's been going on in our lives for the last six months or so. I guess when he and Lila go back to Vegas they're packing their stuff and hitting the road to try to live out his dream of being a mountain man. It's strange because Lila doesn't seem like the type, at least when I first met her, but now she seems different. She seems less preppy, and I hate to say it, but at first I thought she came off as a rich spoiled brat. But she's not though. She's actually really nice.

Ella glances up through her long eyelashes, her gaze skimming over my black jeans, my studded belt, and my Pink Floyd T-shirt, and then she bites her lip. "You look good, too." She closes the journal and sits up. "Trying to impress anyone in particular?"

I roll my eyes and kick a shirt out of the way as I stroll into my room. "Only you."

"Yeah, *I* might know that." She looks down at her hand as she flexes her fingers in front of her and the diamonds and black stone of her engagement ring sparkle. "But unlike me, you don't have a ring on your finger branding you as taken."

"You could always give me my ring," I tell her. "I'll wear it."

She shakes her head, climbs off the bed, and tugs the bottom of her dress down, a dress that looks a lot shorter now that she's standing. "No way. You're not going to see that until the wedding." She pauses, putting her hands on her hips. "It doesn't matter anyway. If any girl hits on you, I'll just kick her ass."

"That's my feisty girl." I give her a deep kiss and then hold up a finger as I get an idea. I back toward the door. "You go out and start having fun and I'll take care of the ring problem."

She looks perplexed but follows me out of the room. She joins the small group gathered in the living room as I head to the door. I slip on my jacket as I step out onto the porch and into the snow. Christmas lights flash from the house across the street and I can hear the thumping of music from somewhere down the street. I trot down the stairs and hurry into the garage, flipping the light on. I pull a box down from the top shelf and set it on the counter. As I'm sifting through the car parts, my phone rings from my pocket. When I take it out, my producer's name, Mike Anderly, flashes across the glowing screen. I press talk and put the phone up to my ear.

"It's a little late to be calling," I tell him, balancing the phone against my ear as I rummage through the box.

"I know, but I couldn't wait until morning to call you and tell you the news," he says, sounding way happier than he normally does. Usually, he's all business and kind of cranky.

"What news?" I pick up the metal ring from the box, smiling at my clever idea.

"That you got on the tour."

I nearly drop the ring. "The Rocking Slam Tour?" I ask. It's the tour I've been trying to get on for months, the one that has a ton of my favorite bands, musicians I idolize. The one where I'll have to be on the road for three straight months.

"That would be the one," he says cheerfully. "So get your ass over here so we can celebrate."

My mouth turns downward. "I can't. I'm in Wyoming, getting ready to get married. I told you this last night."

"Oh yeah, I forgot." He sighs. "Well, hurry and get that taken care of so you can get back here and celebrate. You leave in just a few weeks anyway and we have to finish recording."

Shit. "Yeah . . . I'm not sure I can go."

"What the hell do you mean, you're not sure you can go!" he exclaims. "We've been trying to get you on this tour for months."

"I know that," I tell him. "But I didn't really think it was going to happen, and now I've got stuff going on."

"Well, it did and you're going," Mike says sternly.

"Look, I'm not saying I won't. I'm just saying that I need to talk to Ella first. She needs to be okay with my being gone for that long."

"And what if she says she's not?" he asks, astounded. "Then what?"

"Then I won't go." It hurts to say it, but it's the truth. She's more important to me than anything, and if she doesn't want me to be gone during our first few months of marriage then I won't. It's that simple.

Music starts playing from inside the house and I quickly slip the metal ring on my ring finger, which will hopefully alleviate some of Ella's worry. "Look, I gotta go. I'll call you in a week when I get back in town."

"You better not say no," he grumbles and I hang up the phone before he starts ranting, something he does a lot.

Tucking my phone into my back pocket, I go back inside the house, wondering how Ella is going to react to the news. I can see her pretending like she's okay with it but deep down not really wanting me to go. She hides her feelings well so if I'm going to do this I need to make sure she's completely and utterly okay with it. Any doubt and I'll stay. Besides, as much fun as the tour would be, our little life in San Diego is good, so why ruin a good thing?

Because being part of this tour is my dream.

Frowning at the thought, I shut the back door behind me as I step inside the kitchen. Ethan is sitting on the table, drinking from a red plastic cup and Lila is laughing at something he says while she pours herself a drink over at the counter. There's another couple chatting in front of the kitchen sink. I used to go to school with them, but I can't remember their names. I wave to them when they say "what's up" and then I head for the living room.

"Bottoms up." Ethan lifts his cup as I pass by him, toasting to something, and then he throws his head back and guzzles the drink.

"Are you wasted already?" I ask. "Because you're supposed to play the drums in, like, ten minutes or so."

81

"Nah," he says, but his bloodshot eyes suggest otherwise. "I've got this. Besides, I can play the drums when I'm drunk perfectly fine."

"Micha, do you want me to make you a drink or pour you a shot?" Lila calls out with a bottle of orange juice in her hand.

"No, thanks," I tell her, scooping up a beer from the cooler near the doorway. "I have to stick to beer."

She nods knowingly as she sets the juice down on the counter beside the row of vodka, tequila, and Bacardi bottles and a stack of plastic cups. Ever since Ella called me out on my asshole drunken behavior about a year ago, I take it easier on getting trashed, usually sticking to only a few beers. It was hard at first, but now it's comfortable.

I pop the top off as I stroll into the cigarette-smoke-filled living room, letting the wonderfully potent smoke settle in my lungs. Even a couple of years after kicking the habit, minus a few slipups, it still gets my mouth watering.

Earlier, Ethan and I shoved the couches aside to make room for his drums, which we picked up from his house during our drive back from the grocery store. My old guitar is leaning against a taped together microphone stand. There's also an amp and a bass guitar in the corner beside a small plastic Christmas tree decorated with red and sliver ornaments and tinsel. I haven't figured out who's going to play the bass yet, but I put it up there just in case. I know a lot of people who play the bass and it'd be nice to have a good sound even if it's just a party. I sort of feel like I'm saying good-bye in a way because in a few days I'll be married, my life with Ella will finally start, and this life can hopefully become a memory of everything we shared that got us to that point.

I start to go over to my guitar when I spot Ella sitting on the back of the sofa with a red plastic cup in her hand. A tall, scraggly looking guy whose name I think is Brody is standing in front of the sofa, staring at her legs and cleavage while yammering about something. I walk over to her and hop up on the back of the sofa beside her. Then I drape my arm around her shoulder. I know I'm being territorial and I know she'd never do anything with anyone but it doesn't mean that I'm going to let some guy look at her like he could eat her up. He's lucky I don't punch him. Ella's mine and he needs to walk the fuck away.

"Hey, where'd you go?" Ella asks me as Brody gives me an uneasy look and then walks off without saying a word.

"To get this," I reply, holding up my fingers.

She takes my hand and runs her finger over the

metal ring. "Did you seriously put an O-ring on your ring finger?"

I dazzle her with my most charming smile, the one I know makes her stomach somersault. "Now everyone knows I'm taken."

She takes a sip of her drink and then licks her lips. "Such a shame. I was looking forward to kicking all the girls' asses who hit on you tonight."

"I bet you were," I mumble as I lean forward and lick a drop of alcohol off her lip. "Bacardi, huh?"

She shrugs and angles her head back to take a large swallow. "I thought I'd have fun tonight. Get a little drunk."

I eye her over warily. "I'm not sure I like that. Drunk Ella can sometimes be mean. And horny."

"Hey." She restrains a smile as her hand clamps down on my thigh, squeezing hard. "I'm not a mean drunk."

I waver as I sip my beer. "I can remember a certain tantrum over a lost poker game. One where you drunkenly threw a chip at me."

She narrows her eyes. "Only because you were being smug."

"Smug because I won and got to see you naked."

"Well, maybe I'll get drunk enough tonight that you can see me naked. Just as long as you quit saying I'm a mean drunk." She hops off the couch and my arm falls from her shoulder. "And by the way, you can be the same way when you get drunk."

"What way?"

"Horny and mean."

I raise my beer up and point a finger at it. "That's why I'm sticking to these." I slide my feet off the couch and stand up. "So what song do you want me to play tonight?"

She taps her finger against her lip and there's a playful look in her green eyes. She's already buzzed, which means I'm going to have my hands full tonight. "How about the one tattooed on your ribs? The one you said you wrote for me but I've never heard you play before?"

I automatically touch the side of my rib where the tattoo of the lyrics is hidden underneath the fabric of my shirt. "I've never sung that one out loud for anyone. And I'm not ready to."

"Why not?"

"Because..." I pick at the damp beer label. "Because I wrote it for you."

"Okay..." She frowns, confused. "Then play it for me now."

I glance at the room packed with rowdy and drunk people. "I don't think I can right now."

"Why not?"

"Because it's personal." Because it means so much to me and the last thing I want to do is sing it to a room full of people when I haven't even sung it to her. Besides, I'm a little nervous to sing it for her because it's intense.

She gives me the most lost look and I sigh, because I know I'm acting strange. "It's just that when I wrote it, the lyrics kind of threw me off because it was the first time…that I realized I thought of you…like that."

"But we both know how you feel now," she says, looking at the metallic O-ring on my finger.

"I know that." I stroke her cheekbone with my fingers. "And when I play it for the first time, I want it to be just you and me."

"Like later tonight?" she asks, hopeful.

"Or maybe on our honeymoon," I tell her and smile when her jaw drops. "What? Did you think I didn't have anything planned?"

"But the wedding has been pushed back." She cranes her neck and looks over her shoulder as more people enter the living room. "So if you had one planned, then how'd you move it?"

"Because I had it planned for a few weeks after yesterday, when we were supposed to get married." I suddenly realize that if I go on tour my honeymoon plan has gone to shit. And I saved money to book it, skipping out on eating fast food and instead bringing my lunch—shit like that to get extra cash. A three-day cruise, which is a simple, normal kind of honeymoon and perfect for us since we didn't really do simple or normal for most of our lives.

"So where are we going?" she wonders, intrigued, tucking in her elbow when a guy who I think is named Del walks by wearing a Santa hat and singing "We Wish You a Merry Christmas," drunk off his ass and completely off-key.

"No way. It's a surprise," I say, ushering her toward the front of the room when Ethan waves me over. Standing beside him is Jude Taylorsen, a pretty good bass player, so I'm guessing they're ready to roll. "I have to go play now."

She clutches the cup as she stands in the crowd. It's getting louder and smokier by the second. I know if it gets too packed in here furniture is going to get broken. I didn't use to mind, but now I feel guilty and I make a mental note to kick everyone out before it gets to that point.

"And play that one song," she shouts out as I back up toward where Ethan is chatting it up with Jude. "The one you played at the coffeehouse when I first came back from Vegas."

I smile charmingly at her. "The one where you got all possessive on me?"

She sticks out her tongue. "Kenzie is a skank and a bitch. You should be grateful I saved your ass from that."

I press my hand to my heart. "You were jealous. Admit it."

She glares at me, but her lips itch to turn upward. "I was a little bit."

"I know you were." I wink and start to turn around.

"And if you want, you can play the cover for that song that was playing in the bathroom earlier," she says. "I like that song."

"Like the song?" I question, looking back at her from over my shoulder. "Or like the memory the song's linked to?"

"Both," she says simply and throws her head back to down her drink. The curves of her cleavage peek out of the top of her dress and I shake my head, knowing I'm not the only guy in the room staring at her. But then I smile, knowing I'm the only guy in the room who gets to be with her.

She lowers the cup from her mouth and gives me an accusing look, like she knows I was just staring at her breasts. I blink my gaze off her and head over to the microphone. I set my beer down on the floor next to the wall, pick up my guitar, and slide the strap over my shoulder, running my fingers along the initials I carved in the back. I got the guitar when I was thirteen at a yard sale for, like, five bucks. It was my first guitar and even though it took a bit to get the hang of it, I loved playing it. There's something about music and lyrics that helps me express myself, even when it's hard.

I was playing the first time I realized I had feelings for Ella, feelings that ran much deeper than just friend feelings. She was in the crowd dancing solo like she did a lot, her hands in the air, her hips rocking to the beat. I couldn't take my eyes off her and I found myself wishing I was down there with her, touching and kissing every inch of her. It was that night I went home and wrote the lyrics that I eventually got tattooed on my ribs because it was the kind of moment filled with emotion and the lyrics I created about her needed to be marked on me forever.

It was the moment I realized I loved her, even if I wasn't fully aware of it at the time, but only because I didn't fully understand love yet. Looking back, though, I know the moment I penned the words there'd never be anyone else.

Ella was my one and only.

Chapter Seven

Ella

I refuse to be the sad Ella tonight and dwell on things that aren't making me happy, like my mom, her dark thoughts and fears—*my* dark thoughts and fears. I'm not going to think about my future either or the fact that I can't seem to even get my portfolio started. Tonight it's about having fun and watching Micha play, one of my favorite things in life. I am not going to sink down into a pit.

Micha starts out with the song he sang in the coffeehouse, just like I asked him to do. Sweaty bodies nearly suffocate me as I sway back and forth to the music. Lila's standing beside me, gazing at Ethan pounding on the drums like he's the love of her life. She's wearing a sleeveless blue shirt and jeans, along with a pair of my boots.

"You look starstruck," I shout over the music, fanning my face with my hand, my skin already getting damp with sweat. Even though it's cold as death outside, there are so many people packed in the small living room, the body heat alone makes it desert hot in the house.

She shrugs, her eyes fastened on the front of the room where the guys are playing. "I think I am."

I shake my head and then capture her hand, feeling the alcohol smother any amount of anxiety surfacing. Lila laughs as I spin her around, holding my drink in my hand, ignoring the guy who shouts at me when I accidentally ram my elbow into his gut. Lila grasps onto her drink as she twirls around, trying not to spill any. I keep spinning her until the music stops and Micha's voice flows over the room.

"Okay, this next one was requested by the only person I'll take requests from." He winks at me and some girl shouts out that she'll do whatever he wants if he sings a song for her.

I turn around, scanning the crowd for the culprit and find her at the back of the room. A tall, curvy girl with dark hair, giving me a condescending look as she takes a sip of beer. Kenzie, the waitress from the coffeehouse. Go figure.

"I think someone wants her ass kicked tonight," I state, targeting her with a look. She went to school with me and knows what I'm capable of. It's been a while since I've gotten into a fight, but it doesn't mean I've forgotten how.

Lila claps her hands and jumps up and down. "Oh my God, we should totally take her on together." She turns to me with a smile on her face. "I'll hold her back and you pull her hair."

I gape at her. "Who are you?"

"Someone who wants to find out what it's like to get in a fight." She beams, making fists. "Come on, Ella, be my Mister Miyagi."

"Whoa, you're acting weird and I like it." I tap my finger against my chin thoughtfully. "Well, first off, you don't pull hair. That's a girl's way of fighting."

"But I am a girl."

"Yeah, but if you fight like a guy then you win. Element of surprise. It totally throws them off."

Lila bobs her head up and down, eyeing Kenzie as she takes a swallow from the red cup in her hand. "I could see how that would work."

"It works perfectly almost every time," I assure her. "And if you really want to get mean you can kick—" I'm cut off by the low beat of the drums, guitar, and base mixing together in perfect unison. I turn around and face the front of the room, no longer giving a crap about Kenzie. She can say whatever she wants. It doesn't mean anything to anyone who matters.

Micha strums his long fingers across the guitar as he stands in front of the microphone. His eyes are locked on me, the silver O-ring on his wedding finger glistening in the inadequate light of the living room as he sings the song that was playing while we were in the shower earlier. The lyrics bring fresh memories flooding back and I swear to God I can feel the heat of the steam and the scorching trail his hands left all over my body.

I watch him play, longing to touch him and for him to touch me. I put the plastic cup up to my lips and swallow another mouthful of Bacardi, feeling the burn of it along with the heat on my skin, realizing that Micha was right. I do get horny when I'm drunk because all I can think about right now is him being inside me like he was in the shower.

When his lips part to sing the chorus, I shut my eyes and let the lyrics and sultry sound of his voice spill over my body. I'm gone. The people around me no longer exist. It's just me and Micha and his beautiful voice. I remember the first time I heard him play, sitting in his room on this beanbag chair he had, watching him play and sing on his bed without a shirt on with this intense look on his face, like the words he sang owned him.

"So what do you think?" he'd asked after he'd stopped strumming the strings.

I'd shrugged, pretending that the sketchpad on my lap wasn't holding a drawing of him on the bed. That I didn't just draw him, making lines and shades that mattered. That he mattered enough to me that I took the time to draw him. I felt so lost at the moment, hearing him sing like that as I stared at a drawing that wasn't just a drawing. I was lost but in the most wonderful way.

"It was okay, I guess," I replied nonchalantly, adding a few shadings around his eyes because they were too beautiful not to have extra detail on them.

"Just okay?" He cocked his eyebrow as he held the guitar on his lap. He looked a little upset about my answer and it made me feel guilty.

"No, it was beautiful," I said softly as I stared down at my drawing, uncomfortable at how intimate the moment was because I didn't use the word *beautiful*. Just like I didn't draw pictures of people unless it was an assignment for school.

I waited for him to say something, even though I wished he wouldn't. But he never said anything, finally just playing the same song again. I'd smiled down at my drawing because even though I knew it wasn't possible,

I swear to God he could read my mind and eventually I'd started working on my drawing of him again while listening to him play. I'd always loved music, but hearing it from his mouth warmed my soul in a way that I never knew was possible.

I shake my head from the memory. Maybe there's another sentence to put in my vows. Although, all these notes are getting a little personal and I'm not certain I'll dare read them out loud. Panic claws at my throat and I start to open my eyes to go get another drink, but then Micha reaches the intense part of the song and I don't want to leave the moment. I want to dance, get lost again like the first time I heard him play. So I keep my eyelids closed and sway my hips, shaking my head back and forth, my hair flying everywhere. I'm in heels and it's a struggle to maintain my balance, but I don't care even when I stumble a few times. Just like I don't care that I'm rocking out in a room full of people who are absorbed in beer and trying to find someone to hook up with and who are probably looking at me like I'm a weirdo. I'll take being a weirdo over not enjoying this moment. I've forced myself not to enjoy too many moments in my life. I need more enjoyment. Maybe it's the alcohol in my system that's making me think these things or maybe I'm just being my old self. Or perhaps I'm just being me. Whatever it is, I roll with it, dancing to the tempo of the music. Lila laughs at me and when I open my eyes she's dancing, too.

We continue through the entire song and I keep swaying my hips with my hands above my head, even when the music stops and voices rise around me. Moments later the stereo clicks on and the sound suffocates the chatter. "New Low," by Middle Class Rut, starts vibrating through the speakers and I know it will only be seconds before I'm no longer dancing solo in a room full of people.

Right on cue, Micha's long arms wrap around my waist and he guides me back against his body. I know it's him because of the overpowering scent: his cologne mixed with mint and beer and something intoxicatingly wonderful that belongs only to him. I deeply inhale it in, moving with him as we grind our bodies together to the beat.

"You're so God damn sexy," he says, breathing into my ear and giving it a little nip. "Do you know how hard it is to stand up there and play while you're down here doing this?"

"Doing what?" I ask innocently as his hand sneaks up the back of my dress and cups my bare ass.

His brow arches. "What panties are you wearing?"

I smile to myself. "A sequined thong." I whirl around and press my body up against him, enjoying myself way too much.

His hand slides down my back and he crushes my body into his until there's no space left between us. I roll my hips against him and he lets out a husky growl. Unable to control myself, I throw my arms around him, stand on my tiptoes, and kiss him, urging his lips apart with my tongue. He kisses me with equal intensity as I suck on his lip ring, stroke the inside of his mouth with my tongue, and bite at his bottom lip.

"God damn it, pretty girl, you're killing me." He groans a deep, throaty groan that makes my thighs tingle and I slip my hand between us, rubbing him hard. "Baby, easy. There are people..." He trails off as I move my fingers to the top of his jeans. I know I'm drunk and horny just like he said earlier, but I don't care. I know what I want. Him.

When I start to undo the button of his jeans, he jerks away, his aqua eyes glazed, his expression blazing with desire that matches my own. He doesn't say a word as he entwines our fingers, then pulls me with him as he maneuvers through the crowd for the kitchen, shoving people out of the way with his elbow.

He scoops up two beers as we pass the cooler and hands me one. Ethan is standing beside the cooler, dripping with sweat from playing the drums, his shirt off and his tattoos showing. Lila is behind him with her head on his back as she traces her fingernails up and down his skin.

Micha gives him a chin up and says, "In an hour kick everyone out."

"Why can't you..." Ethan blinks at him and then pulls a face as his gaze flicks between Micha and me while Lila giggles. "All right, will do."

I pinch Micha's ass because I can and he incoherently mutters something. Then he's tugging me with him as he crosses the kitchen and moves toward the hallway. We go into his room and he kicks the door shut behind us. When he turns to face me, his lips immediately cover mine, his fingers digging roughly through the fabric of my dress.

"You taste like beer," I murmur with a drunken giggle as I kiss him back, fiddling with the bottom of his shirt as we back toward his bed with our beers still in our hands.

"And you taste like Bacardi," he mutters against my lips, and then suddenly he's pulling away. "Wait, how wasted are you?"

I roll my eyes. "First of all, even if I were wasted, it wouldn't matter. You can't take advantage of me when I'm yours," I say and this lustful look flares in his eyes. "And second of all, I'm not that wasted. I'll remember everything we did in the morning."

"I do like your logic." He takes the unopened beer from my hand and sets it down on the dresser along with his. "But are you sure?"

"I'm positive."

That's all the convincing he needs. With one swift tug, he jerks my dress over my head so forcefully that he tears the corner of the fabric and sends the pins in my hair flying through the air.

He pulls a "whoops" face, but I cover his mouth with my hand. "It's just a dress." Then I crush my lips against his, his lip ring searing hot against my mouth as my hair falls down and brushes against my shoulders. Minutes later, all our clothes are on the floor and we're lying on his bed, him on his back and me straddling him. He thrusts his hips up to me halfway as I slide down on top of him. His eyes shut as I grip onto his shoulders and I gasp when he sinks farther into me. My hair falls loosely down my back as I slant my head back and shut my eyes. Gripping onto my hips, he rhythmically thrusts inside me over and over again. Our bodies bead with sweat as my mind drifts further away. Helpless energy channels through me and I dig my nails into his flesh, needing something to hold on to. Finally he takes my hands and I grasp on to him until I come apart. I cry out his name and every single worry I had disappears and all that's left is the blissful contentment that only Micha can make me feel.

Chapter Eight

Micha

I'm lying in my bed, thinking about how to tell Ella about the tour when Ethan kicks everyone out of the house. Darkness has settled into my room and the noise and voices slowly dwindle until the house becomes silent. I sit up, but only to turn my iPod on, selecting "I Can Feel a Hot One," by Manchester Orchestra, then lie back down. Ella is naked beside me, flat on her stomach, her hair scattered all over her back, the sheets pulled up halfway over her body as she sleeps soundlessly.

Moonlight flows through the window and across her lower back, highlighting the infinity mark tattooed in black ink. It matches the one on my arm perfectly and sometimes I wish I could remember the night we got them, remember what we'd been thinking when we made the permanent decision. What led up to the moment when we thought, Hey what the hell, let's go get matching tattoos that mean forever and eternally. What was going through our minds? What was going through Ella's mind? I lightly trace the curving lines on her back and I feel her shiver beneath my touch.

"Are you awake?" I ask, my fingers wandering lower, to the top of her ass.

She nods her head, her eyes still closed. "I can't sleep when you're touching me like that."

"How about like this?" I roll over to my side and lean down to kiss her lower back. "Does that help?" I ask, suppressing my laughter when she shivers again.

"No, it's worse, but it's okay. You can keep kissing there if you want to."

I smile to myself and then place another kiss on her back, sliding my tongue over her skin. She squirms so I do it again, then rest my head on her back, place my hand on her side, and my fingers fold around her ribs.

"Do you remember any of that night at all?" she murmurs against the pillow.

"Any of what night?"

"The night we got the tattoos."

"I already told you when we woke up on the park bench that I didn't remember a thing and the memories never came back to me. It's just one of those kinds of nights that I think will be a blank."

"Yeah, but I've always wondered if you were just telling me that you didn't remember because you worried that I'd get weird about whatever happened."

"Well, as much as that sounds like something I'd do, I honestly can't remember a single thing," I say. "Other than, one minute we were drinking a lot out in my backyard while a party went on inside and the next thing I knew we were waking up on the park bench, your shoes were missing, and my arm was burning like a motherfucker. I'd seriously like to know how I managed to convince both of us to do it. And how I managed to get you to do something so permanent," I tell her and she grows quiet, the sound of her breathing mixing with the slow-paced song. The longer she remains silent, the more I start to worry. "Ella May?"

"Yeah." Her voice is high and full of nervousness.

My palm glides down her side to her hips. "Have you been lying about not remembering any of that night?"

She pauses, her body tensing. "No. I've already told you a thousand times I can't remember a thing."

"Pretty girl, I think your lie's showing." I tickle her side and she buries her face in the pillow, shaking her head. "You do remember something, don't you?"

I press my chest against her back and lean over her shoulder, dipping my mouth to her ear. "Just tell me. I won't be mad."

"I know you won't be mad," she says, rotating her head to the side so her face is away from the pillow. "But you'll be smug, which is worse and why I've kept it a secret."

"I won't be smug," I say enticingly. "I promise."

"You will too, Micha Scott," she argues. "I know you too well not to think otherwise."

"I can make you roll over and tell me." I push away from her a little and skim my finger down her back to the center of her legs. She jumps, startled, as I start to put my finger inside her.

"Micha." She narrows her eyes through the dark as she flips over onto her back and bolts upright, the moonlight hitting her bare chest. "That was a low move."

I sit up, pulling her legs over my lap as I turn to the side and relax against the wall. Then I situate her on my lap, so her ass is positioned over my cock. "Just tell me," I say. "I'll try not to be smug but I want to know."

She sighs and then puts her head against my shoulder. "Fine, but only because I love you."

I kiss her forehead, breathing in her words, never getting tired of hearing them. "Fair enough."

She sighs again and then she splays her fingers across my stomach. "You remember how we decided that everyone at your house was annoying and that we just needed to have a party of our own so we took a bottle of Bacardi and snuck outside?"

I nod, resting my chin on top of her head. "Everyone was always annoying."

"Yet you always had the parties." She draws a pattern across my stomach and then up to my chest. "Almost every weekend after you turned sixteen."

"I was bored and liked the distraction." I shiver from her touch—she's the only girl who's ever gotten me to shiver.

She walks her fingers up my stomach and stops them over my heart, pressing her palm flat against it. "The distraction from what?"

I place my hand over hers and trap her hand in place. "From you."

She tenses and so do I because I know what's coming.

"Is that why you slept around so much?" she asks quietly.

I shut my eyes, knowing she can feel the acceleration in my heart rate. "Haven't I always told you I was just passing time until you came around?"

"Yeah, but did you really have to sleep with everyone?"

"I didn't sleep with everyone—not even close," I point out. "And I was sixteen and horny and everyone I hung around with was having sex."

"So it was because of peer pressure?" she questions doubtfully. "Because that doesn't sound like you."

I open my eyes and sigh, releasing her hand. "It wasn't really because of anything and that's kind of the point. I was young and bored and in love with my best friend and if I tried to do anything at all that went past the friend boundary, she'd get upset. I didn't know what to do with myself half the time, and honestly, Ella, I felt like shit most of the time about the stuff I did, not just with other girls but with you." I pause, giving her room to say something and when she doesn't, I continue. "Do you remember that time when I made you go racing with me and when I won I kissed you because I got a little overly excited?"

She hesitantly nods with her hand still positioned over my heart. "I almost punched you in the face, but only because it was a reflex. I wasn't used to people touching me like that."

"You were so pissed."

"Only because I was confused."

I pause. "About what?"

She hesitates. "About me and you and what I was feeling."

"And what were you feeling? Because I'm dying to know." Even though I have her now, I still love hearing about our past and the fact that sometimes I wasn't the only one suffering in silence.

She turns her face toward me so her breath warms my chest, her lips grazing my skin. "I'm not sure."

"Did you like what you were feeling?" I touch my lips to her forehead.

She wavers for a moment and then nods. "I did. A lot. And that was the problem."

I smile as I stare over her head at the window where Christmas lights glow through the darkness outside. There's a set of silver ones on the tree that leads to Ella's room, the one I used to climb up all the time just so I could be near her. "Thank you, pretty girl."

"For what?"

"For telling me that. It's nice to hear that it wasn't always me," I say. "Now will you please tell me about the tattoos?"

She grimaces and then moves her head back to look me in the eyes. "It was my idea to go get them," she admits.

My jaw nearly drops. "What?"

She rolls her eyes at herself and then sits up, swinging her leg over me so she's straddling my lap and her nipples brush against my bare chest. "We were drunk and you dared me to kiss you so I did. And then I stupidly suggested that it would be super funny if we did something to mark the moment and then decided it should be tattoos."

"And I just willingly went with you?" I ask, not with skepticism because it does sound like something I'd do.

She nods as her palms glide up my shoulders and then she links her arms around the back of my neck, her soft nipples grazing my chest. "You took me over to Jason's house and asked him to put infinity marks on us."

"And then what?" I inquire, my fingers finding her waist.

She shrugs. "And then that's where things get a little hazy."

I consider what she said and it makes me happy. "So this entire time you were the reason I have this on me." I raise my arm with the infinity mark on it.

She sketches it with her finger. "Does it make you mad?"

"No, it kind of makes me very, very happy."

"Why?"

"Because it proves that you might have loved me all along."

She wets her lips with her tongue and then leans into me, so close that when she blinks, her eyelashes brush against mine. "Even though I didn't know it at the time," she whispers against my lips, "I think you're right and I'm glad I finally figured it out."

Chapter Nine

Ella

Even though I can feel it in my bones that I should stop, the next morning I read some more of my mother's journal. The part I'm reading was written a little before her wedding and she doesn't seem happy about it at all. She seems depressed and sad and everything a soon-to-be wife shouldn't be.

> *I'm not sure I can do it. Go down to the courthouse and make it official. I'd rather claw my eyes out. If my mother had her way, I wouldn't go through with it. She says Raymond is no good, that he'll ruin my life, and that I'm not fit to be a mother or a wife right now especially with what I've been going through...the drastic mood swings, the ups and downs. She's probably*

right, but then again I feel like my life is already ruined, whether I'm married and a mother or not. Besides, I really do think I might love Raymond. Maybe. But sometimes the mere thought of taking another breath seems like the biggest chore in the world. I wish I could stop breathing. I wonder if it's possible for someone to be able to hold their breath long enough to die.

Maybe I should try.

I look over at the picture of her and the drawing of the flower in the vase. When did she draw this and when was the picture taken? When she wrote this? Before? After? Why am I obsessing over it so much? *Just let it go.*

"Baby, are you ready for this?" Micha asks as he loops his leather belt through the top of his worn jeans.

Tensing, I close the journal, noting that he hesitantly glances at it. "Yeah, as ready as I'll ever be."

"It'll be fine." He fastens his belt, then reaches for the cologne, glancing at the journal again as I climb off the bed. "Are you going to ask your dad about the journal?"

"Yeah, I guess now is as good a time as any." I'm wearing a black and purple plaid shirt and jeans that are tucked into boots. I comb my fingers through my tangled hair and reach for my deodorant that's in my duffel bag. "I just hope he doesn't act all weird about it."

Micha sets the cologne back down on the dresser beside a pile of his old guitar picks. "Why would he act weird about it?"

I shrug, removing the cap from my deodorant. "Because it has to do with my mom, and what if he wants to read it?"

"Then let him read it."

I wipe some deodorant on my armpits and then toss it back into the bag. "Yeah, but it says stuff...about him...not nice stuff either, at least not great stuff about how she felt about marrying him."

His throat bobs up and down as he swallows hard, raking his fingers through his hair. "Yeah, maybe you shouldn't then." He pulls open the top dresser drawer and begins digging through it like he's looking for something when there are only a few old T-shirts in there.

I touch his arm lightly. "Micha?"

He stiffens under my touch. "Yeah."

"I want to marry you more than I've wanted to do anything else in my life," I say, turning him so that he's facing me, even though he's got his head tipped down. "And yes, I know that sounds super cheesy, but it's true so..." I trail off as he leans in toward me.

"Even after everything you've been reading?" he asks, his hand cupping the side of my neck.

I nod and his mouth covers mine. I part my lips as his tongue devours me in a deep, passionate kiss, his fingers knotting through my hair, tugging at the roots, forcing my head back. When he pulls away he looks high on the kiss, eyes glazed, pupils wide, and I love him for it.

"There is something I want to talk to you about," I tell him, because I know it's time to ask questions that need to be asked. To have the talk about where we'll be in a few years, what our plans are for the future. "But let's do it after we tell my mom and your dad that we're getting married."

"Are you sure?" he asks, his fingers unraveling through my hair.

"I'm sure," I say. "Besides, if we don't get this whole wedding announcement thingy out in the open there isn't going to be a wedding, at least one that people can go to."

"Where are we going to have it?"

"I don't know," I say, and I don't. Even when I was little, I never imagined getting married. In fact, when I thought about it, I thought about how much I didn't want it. I watched my mother and father fight too much, be miserable, fall apart, our household always on the verge of cracking until one day it shattered completely. But I've changed. And it doesn't matter where it takes place or what I'm wearing. I just want Micha there with me and I'm good. "In your backyard?" I suggest. "I mean, a lot of stuff happened in the backyard."

His sucks on his lip ring, contemplating. "Yeah, a lot of things did, but a lot of things happened at our spot, too, so how about up by the lake. It's where we first said we loved each other, even if you don't remember it."

"Won't it be cold?"

"Does it really matter?"

He has a point, but I still frown at the floor, my heart knotting in my chest as I remember the night on the bridge and how I almost jumped into the water. How Micha saved me. How I kissed him afterward to silence the three words I knew he was going to utter, words I can't get enough of now. I remember turning to leave, ready to bolt from him and my feelings, and then the rest of the night is only broken pieces in my mind because of the mixture of adrenaline and anxiety in my body, along with the pills I took from my mother's stash. Rain drops splashing against the asphalt. Puddles covering the ground. Water like black ink. Silver lightning blazing across the midnight sky. Micha's intoxicating warmth. "You never did tell me

exactly what happened." I glance up at him. "Would...
would you tell me what happened? I want to know
what happened the night I first told you I loved you."

He looks at me for what feels like an eternity,
assessing me as he contemplates what I've asked. Then
instead of walking out of the room like I fear, he pulls
me down onto the bed with him and wraps his arms
around me. "Absolutely. I'll always give you whatever
you want."

Chapter Ten

Two and a half years earlier . . .

Micha

Rain hammers down from the sky and slams against the charcoal asphalt, soaking my jeans and T-shirt. Lightning zaps across the sky and thunder booms, reverberating through the metal beams around and above the bridge. My lips are numb from the cold air, Ella's kiss, and the fact that she's walking away from me.

"Ella May, don't you dare run away from this," I yell as I jog after her, my boots splashing against the puddles.

She's having a hard time walking, veering from left to right as the rain drenches her jeans, shirt, and hair. The beams of the headlights from my car parked in the center of the bridge light up the darkness and makes her look like a shadow. "Micha, just leave me alone. *Please.*" She trips over her feet and falls to the ground.

I don't know if it's from the pills she took, if she's been drinking, if it's the combination of the two, or the simple fact that she's having a panic attack.

I speed up and wrap my arms around her waist. As I help her to her feet, she wiggles her arms and tries to jab me with her elbows, attempting to shove me away.

"Just let me go!" she cries and I hear a sob in her voice. It splits my heart into pieces because she never cries. *Ever*. The pain she's feeling…God, I can't even think about it. "Please just let me go."

"No," I say as I support her weight in my arms and help her back to my car. "I'm never going to let you go. Don't you get that?"

Holding on to her with one hand, I maneuver the passenger door open as rain continues to drown us. I put my hand over her head and help her duck down into the car. Once she's sitting in the seat and the door is shut, I feel slightly better, the crushing weight in my chest lighter. Not gone, but lighter than when I pulled up and found her standing on the edge of the bridge.

I blink through the rain as I look over at the beam Ella was balancing on and then at the dark water below. "God damn it!" I curse and kick the tire as I yank my fingers through my wet hair. How did everything turn this shitty? How could a beautiful, smart, wildly wonderful girl be handed so many shitty fucking cards?

She's spent most of her life taking care of her parents, and then her mother takes her own life and her father blames her. Why does she have to deal with this? Why can't something good finally happen to her?

I have no idea how to handle this, but I know I have to try. Forcing my feet to move around the front of the car, I get into the driver's seat and slam the door. "It's fucking cold in here," I say, cranking up the heat as my wet clothes soak the leather seat.

She doesn't look at me, keeping her forehead against the window and her hands lifelessly on her lap as rain drips from her hair onto her cheeks. "I can't feel anything," she mumbles.

My heart sinks inside my chest and I have to take a slow breath before I speak. "Baby, put your seat belt on."

She shakes her head, her eyes shutting. "I...can't..." She sounds exhausted, on the verge of passing out.

I lean over and reach across the front of her. When I grab the seat belt, she doesn't budge even when I pull it over her chest. As I'm buckling her in, she abruptly shifts her weight toward me. The seat belt clicks into the lock as she rests her forehead against mine, her skin as cold as the rain outside.

"You almost...you almost said you love me..." Her warm breath hits my skin as her eyes stay shut.

"I know." I swallow hard, but I'm still afraid to move and break the connection between us. Water drips down my forehead, across my lips, and runs from my hand as I move my fingers away from the buckle and to her hip.

"No one's ever said that to me before," she whispers.

"I know," I say, my fingers shaking as I hold on to her.

Her shoulder turns inward and presses into mine as she slumps more of her weight into me. "Did you . . . did you mean it?"

I slowly nod without leaning away, causing friction between our foreheads. "More than anything."

"Micha I . . ." she starts and my chest aches for her to say it. *Just say it please.* But then her forehead is leaving mine and she's moving back toward the door. "I'm really tired," she whispers, slumping her head against the window again.

I gradually inhale and then release, trying to steady my erratic heart. It takes more than a few breaths to get me to where I can even speak again. "I'll take you home."

"No, not home," she utters. "Somewhere else . . . I hate home . . ."

I turn forward in my seat and watch the raindrops crash down against the hood and windshield. "Where do you want to go?"

118

"Somewhere that will make me happy," she says and flinches when thunder booms.

Placing my hands on top of the steering wheel, I shut my eyes. Some place that will make her happy? I'm not sure a place like that exists at the moment, but I have to try. Opening my eyes back up, I shove the shifter into reverse and back up off the bridge. When I reach the end, I put it into drive and crank the wheel, turning the car around.

The road is flooded with puddles and the windshield wipers are cranked on high as I drive away from the bridge. Every time the thunder and lightning snaps, I jump, but Ella stays still, nearly motionless. When she does move, it's only to mess around with the iPod. She skims through the song list forever, her fingers fumbling over the buttons. She keeps shivering but when I ask her if she's cold she shakes her head. Finally she selects a song: "This Place Is a Prison," by The Postal Service. Then she slouches back in the seat, leans her head back against the headrest, and stares at the ceiling as the song plays through the speakers.

I continue to drive until I reach the side road that weaves out to a secluded area surrounded by trees and nestled near the edge of the lake. The road is a muddy mess and I'm worried that we're going to get stuck. But somehow I manage to make it to our spot, the one Ella and I always go to be alone—to be with each other. I park the car so it's facing the dark water and leave the headlights on. The water ripples against the raindrops as the wipers move back and forth across the windshield.

"Tell me what you're thinking?" I finally say, not staring at the lake.

"I'm thinking I should have jumped," she says emotionlessly.

Something snaps inside me and I lose it. "No, you fucking don't!" I ram my fist against the top of the wheel and she jumps, lifts her head up, and stares at me with wide eyes. "You don't want to be dead, so stop saying it." My voice softens as I reach over and tuck strands of wet hair behind her ear. "You're just confused."

"No, I'm not," she protests. "I know exactly what I'm thinking." But I can tell she doesn't by the glossiness of her eyes, the vastness of her pupils, and the fact that she's struggling to keep her eyelids open. "I don't want to be here anymore, Micha."

"With me?" I choke, cupping her cheek.

She swallows hard, her eyes scanning mine. "I don't know."

"But I thought you knew exactly what you were thinking?" I say, not sure if I'm going about this the right way, but it's the only way I know how.

"All I know is that I don't want to feel this." She slams her hand over her chest, a little too hard. Her eyes are wildly big, filled with fear and panic as her chest heaves for air. "I don't want to feel all this pain and guilt."

"What happened to your mother wasn't your fault." I place a very unsteady hand over hers, worried I'm going to fuck this up. I'm stunned by how rapidly her heart is beating, thrashing against our hands. She's probably got so much adrenaline pouring through she's lightheaded.

"That's not what my dad and Dean say," she whispers, pulling her hand away and forcing mine to fall from her chest.

"Your dad and your brother are fucking assholes," I tell her firmly, leaning over the console. "And it doesn't matter what they think—no one else matters but you and me. Remember, you and me against the world."

Her eyelids shut and then flutter open again. "You're always saying that."

"Because I mean it. I don't care about anything else. I could lose anyone else and make it through. But not you, Ella May. I can't do this without you."

A few tears fall down her cheeks. "I hate myself."

"Ella, God damn it, don't say—"

"No!" she shouts, jerking away from me and huddling against the door. "I fucking hate myself! I do! And I wish you'd just see what I really am. You're always seeing more in me than what there really is..." She drifts off as more tears spill out and she scans the outside of the car, the trees, the water, the rain, like she's contemplating running. "If you'd just let me go, you'd be happier."

"No, I wouldn't." I ball my hands to keep from touching her because I know it's going to set her off more. "I..." I blow out an uneven breath, knowing that what I'm about to say is going to change everything, even if she won't remember it in the morning. I will. I can't go back from it and honestly I don't fucking want to. "I fucking love you. Don't you get that?" I unclench my hands and stretch my arm over to her, grabbing her arm as she shakes her head. "I love you." My voice softens. "And no matter what happens, with you or me—with us—I'm *always* going to love you."

Her shoulders start to heave and she gives in to my hold, allowing me to pull her over the console and onto my lap. Then I wrap my arm around her and cradle her head against my chest as she sobs into my wet shirt. I smooth my hand down her head, each sob tearing at my heart. I stare out into the rain, watching it splash against the lake, feeling so helpless. I wish I could take all of her pain and guilt away. She doesn't deserve this—she doesn't deserve anything. What she does deserve is someone to love her unconditionally, which I've been trying to do for a while, if she'd just let me. *I need to find a way.*

"Micha." The sound of her strained voice jerks me back to reality.

When I glance down at her, she's looking up like she's lost and has no idea where she is as she clutches onto my shirt. I know she's probably going to fall asleep soon and when morning rolls around there's a good chance she won't remember any of this.

I trace a finger underneath her eyes, wiping the tears away. "Yeah, baby?"

She takes a deep breath and then she's pulling on my shirt, forcing me to get close to her. "I love you, too," she whispers and then she presses her lips against mine. She kisses me briefly, but it's enough that I feel it all the way through me. I clutch on to her as I kiss her back with every ounce of emotion I have in me, wishing it could be just like this all the time. But just as quickly as it all began, it stops as she leans away and settles back in my arms. Moments later, she's asleep.

I listen to the rhythm of her breathing and the longer I sit there holding her, the fiercer my heart beats, and no matter how hard I try to keep them back, eventually tears escape my eyes. My head falls forward against the steering wheel and I cry quietly through the sounds of the rain. Crying for her. For the life she was handed. Because I'm so in love with her it hurts me to see her like this. Because I know when morning comes, there's a good chance she won't remember this.

Because I'm afraid I'm going to lose her forever.

Chapter Eleven

Ella

When Micha finishes telling me what happened, I lay quietly on the bed with him, my head right over his heart. It's beating faster than it normally does and I wonder if he's feeling what he felt that night. The fear I put in him and whatever else was going through his head at the moment.

"I can't remember any of that," I say, looking up at him. "I think it was the combination of the pills and my... my anxiety. Things sometimes get blurry when I go to that place."

"I know," he says, staring down at me. "Like I said, I knew that night there would be a good chance you wouldn't remember any of it. I just thought that I'd never see you again after it happened."

Silence stretches between us as I struggle to remember and he struggles to forget.

"I'm sorry," I tell him because it's the only thing I can think of to say. There are no words that could possibly even begin to explain to him how bad I feel for putting him through that and for me doing it to begin with. It still hurts to even think about it, how I was about to throw everything away—everything I have with Micha now. "I really am."

He moves me with him as he sits up. "You don't have to be sorry for something that happened a few years ago—something that wasn't even in your control."

"Running away was."

"You know, I thought so at first, but now I don't think that's entirely true. I think sometimes in life shit happens and people have to do what they can to move past it." The corners of his mouth tug upward into a sad smile. "For you, that was running away and for me…with my father, it was deciding it was better to let him go."

"But I came back." I tuck my legs under me and kneel up between his legs. "Well, I came back for summer break because I had to, but now I'm back, for the most part."

"I know." His fingers spread across my cheek. "It's called healing, Ella May."

"I guess it is," I agree. "But you wouldn't let your father back into your life, even if he tried."

His thumb grazes my bottom lip. "I've got everyone I need in my life. My mom. You. Even Ethan and Lila. That's more than a lot of people have." His hand leaves my lips and he threads his fingers through mine so the O-ring on his finger is pressed against my engagement ring. "Besides, I have you forever. And one day we'll have our own family and that's what will matter in the end."

I'm not sure what kind of face I make, but he definitely notes a shift as I move to the edge of the bed.

"What's wrong?" he asks, sitting up straight and sliding his long legs over the edge of the bed and his feet onto the floor.

I wanted to prepare myself for this talk, about our future, where we're going, but now it's kind of unavoidable because he said our own family…Shit. Does he mean kids and everything? "I've actually been meaning to talk to you about that."

"About what? Having you forever, or having a family of our own?"

"Um…" I swallow hard. "The last part."

"About having a family." He speaks slowly and cautiously like he's afraid he's going to scare me.

"Yeah, sort of…" I struggle to talk about a subject that makes me feel so uneasy. "I mean, where are we even going?"

127

He looks puzzled. "I'm not sure I'm following you, pretty girl."

"Are we..." God, this is so difficult. "When you say family, are you...are you talking about having kids?"

He considers his next words wisely. "Not having kids right at this moment, but having them in the future, yeah."

"And what if...what if I said I didn't want to have kids?" I bring my feet back onto the bed and sit cross-legged.

He scratches his scruffy jawline as he brings his feet up on the bed and faces me, crisscrossing his legs. "It all depends on why you don't want to have them, I guess."

"So you do want to have them?" I'm a little surprised that he doesn't even have to think about it.

His eyes search mine and then he definitively nods. "Not right now, but eventually way down the road."

"And what if I said that way down the road I couldn't see myself as a mother?" I chew on my lip nervously. "Then what?"

He slips his fingers through mine and holds both of my hands. "Why can't you see yourself as a mother?"

I roll my eyes and pull one of my hands away to gesture at myself. "I think it's sort of obvious."

He looks genuinely perplexed. "No, not really."

"Because of who I am." I struggle for words. "Because of my problems. Because I don't even know what being a mother entails. I mean, I had a few good moments growing up, but other than that I pretty much took care of my mother instead of the other way around."

He wiggles his fingers from my hand, grabs my knees, and drags me closer to him. "Exactly, which is why I think you'll make a great mom."

"I think you're wrong," I disagree. "If anything, it'll make me a very confused mom."

His hands glide from my knees to my thighs and his fingers jab into my skin like he's afraid to let me go. "No way. As much as I hate it, you took care of everyone in that household. You cooked. Cleaned. Paid the bills. Helped your mom take her medication. Stayed home and took care of her while your father went out to the bar every night acting like a teenager. At sixteen, Ella May, you were more responsible than a lot of thirty-year-olds."

"I did stupid stuff, too," I remind him. "I think you're forgetting all the fights I got into, all the roofs I jumped off, the many times I made you drive recklessly and tested the boundaries of life."

"You had to breathe somehow."

I think about what he said, squirming because

all this positive talk about me is making me uneasy. "You're seriously freaking me out right now."

"I know," he says. "But it's the truth. You'll make an awesome mom if and when that time comes around."

I eye him over with skepticism. "And what if it doesn't? What if I say there's just no way I can do it? What if I say that I just want to spend the rest of my life drawing and listening to you sing? Just you and I?"

"Then I guess it'll be just you and I growing old together," he says with a trace of a smile on his lips. "And I can live with that, too. I can live with anything just as long as you fucking marry me." And with that, he gets to his feet. "This weekend. No more messing around." He sticks out his hand and I take it, nodding.

He pulls me to my feet and we walk toward the door. "Although, I must say that we would make beautiful babies together." He flashes me a cocky grin and I roll my eyes. "Imagine one with your hair and my amazing eyes."

"You're too cocky for your own good. Besides, I'd rather they had your hair and my eyes. I've never been a fan of the color." My face twists in disgust I grab a few strands. "Although I love your eyes, too. Maybe she could just have your hair *and* eyes."

His brow crooks up as he starts to pull the door open "She?"

I bite down on my tongue, realizing my slipup. "Did I say 'she'?" I feign dumb.

He nods and there's a sparkle in his aqua eyes as we step out into the hallway. "So you'd want a girl?"

I fight for oxygen and then seal my lips. If I could picture myself with a kid, I picture her as a little girl, all punked out with blonde hair and blue eyes. I'm not ready to admit that aloud yet, though. "Can we just go tell your mom about the wedding?" I ask, trying to sound neutral, but my voice comes out more off pitch than I intended. "Before Lila and Ethan let it slip out."

He looks at me for about five seconds longer and I wonder who he sees. The girl he met when he was four? Or the one who ran away when she was eighteen? Or this new one who thinks about weddings and babies? "Whatever you want," he finally says and starts down the hall.

He's always saying that and I tug on his arm, stopping him. "What about what you want for once?"

He pauses, searching my eyes for God knows what. "I have everything I want right here," he says simply, and I can tell he means it.

Chapter Twelve

Micha

The whole baby talk with Ella was a little weird, but it needed to be talked about, I guess. I'd never thought that much about it, but having kids wouldn't be so bad, down the road of course. It's not like I worry I'd turn into a shitty father like mine. I think I was always a bit more like my mom than him and I'm glad. But I want to make sure that Ella and I are both in the right place if we decide to have them.

I meant everything I said. Either way, kids or not, I'll be happy as long as I'm with her. But I think now I really need to talk to her about my future in music and the tour coming up. I should have probably told her right after the baby talk since we were talking about our future. It would have been a good time, but I was scared and nervous of what she would say—or what she wouldn't say. Music is my passion, my emotional outlet in really hard times, and Ella knows this and I know she'll be supportive, but what I don't know is if she'll come with, and if she does, will she be doing it because she wants to or because she thinks it's what I want? And if she doesn't, then that means I have to give it up—give up my dream. And knowing that makes me want to avoid it as long as possible.

With the tour and our future still lingering in my mind, we enter the kitchen with our fingers linked, the fresh aroma of coffee in the air. I feel like I'm seven years old again and Ella and I are telling my mom how we broke our next-door-neighbor Mrs. Millerson's garden gnome because we wanted to see if it was a real gnome. Mrs. Millerson had caught us and told us we had to get her a new one. We thought we were going to get yelled at but thankfully my mom always went a little easy on me due to the fact that my dad bailed out and she's always had a soft spot for Ella.

But now instead of telling my mom about the broken gnome we're telling her that we want to have a wedding in five days and how we almost got married without her. My mom flips out at first, more than I thought she would, but her anger turns to excitement when I remind her that yeah, we were going to get married without her but we decided not to.

Thomas, my mom's boyfriend who's a little younger

than her, is in the kitchen eating a bowl of cereal at the table while all this goes on. He looks a little more cleaned up than when we last saw him; at least he's wearing a clean T-shirt and jeans without holes in them. My mom is still dressing like she's younger—her shirt has all this flashy diamond shit on it and there's some on the trim of her pants. But I don't say anything about it. I get that she's happy and even though I still think Thomas is an idiot, especially when he drips milk on the front of his shirt, he seems to make her happy.

"So we're really going to do this?" my mom asks with a grin on her face as she pours a cup of coffee.

"Do what?" I ask, exchanging a confused glance with Ella, who shrugs, as confused as I am.

My mom shakes her head at me as she sets the coffee-pot down on the counter near the sink. "Get married."

I press back a smirk. "I didn't realize it was a *we* thing."

She sighs, like I'm a silly little child, and walks past us, making her way across the kitchen to the fridge. "I didn't mean *we* as in all of us." She opens the fridge door and takes out a gallon of milk. "I meant *we* as in you and Ella." She beams at Ella as she pours milk into her coffee. "The daughter I never had. God, this is going to be so much fun."

Ella steps back, tensing, shying away because my

mom's enthusiasm is scaring the shit out of her. "What's going to be so much fun?" she asks.

"Planning your wedding." My mom glances at Ella and me as she puts the milk back into the fridge. "You two are going to have the best wedding. I'm going to make sure of that."

I pull Ella toward me and circle my arms around her waist, trying to ease her panic. "You know you have only five days to plan it and then we have to return home, right?" I tell my mom.

My mom clasps her hands together and glances over her shoulder at the snowflakes drifting down from the cloudy sky. It's early afternoon but with the lack of sunlight it looks like it's late in the day. "Five days is perfect." She returns her attention to us. "I can do a lot in five days."

"And we're all broke," I remind her, pressing Ella's back against my chest. She's being really quiet and it's making me nervous. I'm not sure if it's all the wedding talk that's freaking her out or the fact that we just had a baby talk.

"I have some money saved up." My mom collects her cup of coffee from the counter. "And besides, you can have a nice wedding without spending a whole lot of money." Her eyes land on Ella. "Do you have a dress already?"

Ella shakes her head and then blinks at my mom distractedly. "What?"

"A dress, sweetie." My mom looks at me questioningly from over the top of her cup as she takes a swallow. "Does she have one yet?"

I lean over Ella's shoulder to catch her eye and I'm startled by the layer of water in her eyes. There's something wrong and I need to find out what it is. "Yeah, she has one," I say to my mom and then grab Ella's hand and lead her toward the hallway, calling over my shoulder. "Mom, we'll be right back."

Ella absentmindedly follows me. Once I get her into the hallway and out of my mother's gaze, I stop us and whirl her around to face me.

"Okay, what's wrong?" I ask, examining her watery eyes.

She stares over my shoulder at a few framed pictures of my mom and me hanging on the wall. "It's nothing."

I place my hand on her cheek and force her to look at me. "It is something; otherwise you wouldn't be about ready to cry."

"I don't..." Tears bubble in the corner of her eyes and her voice cracks. "It's just that...God, this is so stupid." She rubs the tears from her eyes with the back of her hand.

"Nothing you say is stupid," I assure her, wiping a stray tear away with my thumb.

She frowns doubtfully at me. "Even when I told you that I was pretty sure we could push to one hundred miles per hour when there was a foot of snow on the road?"

"Yeah, well, we all have our drunk moments," I say, recollecting the night she's talking about. How she was a little drunk and a little excited over the fact that some dude told her she had a nice ass. She would never admit that was what was making her all cheery, but I could tell it was and it was fucking annoying.

"Go faster," she'd begged from the passenger seat with her head against the dashboard as she watched the night sky through the window. "Go, like, a hundred."

"No way," I'd replied, shifting into a lower gear as the engine grumbled. The road was dangerous going twenty-five, the car barely able to keep any sort of traction as we slid up the vacant street, heading home.

"Oh come on, Micha Scott." She sat up and ran her fingers through her hair. She had on a leather jacket and a black shirt underneath it that had a low collar and I could see the curves of her breasts. The sight made me hard, which pissed me off because another guy had put a smile on her face. "Just try it. If things get too crazy, you can stop."

I shook my head, ripping my gaze from her cleavage. "You're drunk and thinking stupid."

"Hey, that's not very nice." She'd pouted. I hated when she pouted because she looked ridiculously sexy and it made it difficult to deny her anything she was asking for, even if it meant us getting killed. She propped her elbows onto the console and leaned over, putting her face only inches away from my cheek. "Come on, just do it. For me." She had this amused, drunk look on her face. She was too gorgeous, perfect, beautiful for her own good. If I could, I would have told her that. Told her how amazingly perfect she was and how I could spend thousands of hours writing lyrics about how beautiful she was and it wouldn't even begin to describe it.

My eyes may have been on the road but all my attention was on her. "Pretty girl, I'm not going to kill us, no matter how hard you beg."

Her lip popped out even more as she slumped back in the seat. "Fine. Don't have any fun." Propping her boots on the console, she'd slouched back against the seat. "And I don't know why you keep calling me that."

"What, pretty girl?" I smiled amusedly as she nodded with a frown, her eyelids drifting shut as exhaustion took her over. I took a chance, telling her the truth, knowing that she probably wouldn't remember it by morning. "It's because I think you're beautiful, but I can never get away with calling you beautiful without you kicking my ass, so I settled for a milder version of the truth." I sighed as she passed out, her knees slumping to the side and falling off the dash and onto the floor. Then her head lowered down against the console and she wiggled it to the side until it was pressed against my ribs and her hair was on my lap. Smiling, I slowed down the car and took my time getting home. The night actually turned out to be pretty fucking perfect.

"I've had a lot more stupid moments than you." Ella's voice jerks me from the memory.

"Oh, I doubt that," I argue, bracing my hand on the wall beside her head. "And I doubt that whatever you're going to tell me is going to sound stupid."

She rubs her hand over her face, leaving red lines on her skin. "Part of the reason..." She clears her throat. "I'm just thinking about mom stuff. That's all."

"About the journal?"

"No...about getting married...without a mom around." She wavers. "It's part of the reason why I wanted to get married here. So we would be close to her."

My heart sinks into my stomach. Through all of

this, I'd never even thought about that. About how she must be feeling about her mom not being around for all of this.

"See, I told you it was stupid," she says with a heavyhearted sigh. "I should just keep my mouth shut."

"No, it's not stupid. Not at all." I pause, considering my next words carefully because they're important. "Do you want to have it somewhere near the cemetery?"

She quickly shakes her head. "No, I like by the lake. It's just nice knowing she's in the same town. God, this is so weird. I'm talking about her like she's still alive." Her voice quivers at the end and she looks away, avoiding eye contact with me.

"Hey." With my hand, I turn her head back toward me. "Nothing about wanting your mother near you is weird, whether she's alive or not."

She smiles sadly, but it's nice to see her smile while we're talking about her mom, even if it's a sad smile. "Well, I still want to have it at the lake," she tells me. "And my dad will be there, so I guess it won't be so bad."

"What about Dean and Caroline?" I ask. "Should we invite them?"

"Caroline's pregnant so I'm not even sure she could and it's super short notice," she says.

"It's up to you." I give her a quick kiss on the lips and then step back. "If you don't want to invite them, then fine. But, I mean, you do get married only once, you know."

Her lips creep into a malicious grin. "Oh, I plan on getting married a lot. At least ten to twenty times. You're just my practice husband." She playfully nudges me with her shoulder.

I embrace her and catch her off guard as I tackle her to the floor like I used to when we were kids. My hand snaps out before we hit the carpet and I catch her weight. Then I hold my body up slightly away from her so I don't crush her.

"Micha." She laughs, her legs opening up so my body falls in between them. Her fingers span across my shoulder blades as I press on her lower back, our legs entangled. "Get off me. We're too old for this."

"No way," I say. Heat radiates between our bodies and her hair is sprawled around her head and across the carpet, and the tears that were in her eyes moments ago are gone. "We'll never be too old for this. Ever. I will still tackle you when we're ninety years old."

She stares up at me for a moment, her expression unreadable, her pulse hammering through her fingertips. "You make me happy," she says in a shaky voice.

It may seem like such a simple statement, but for Ella to admit she's happy is a huge, major, life-changing event and it gives me hope that everything will end up okay.

"And vice versa," I say and then kiss her.

Chapter Thirteen

Ella

Telling Micha's mom was a piece of cake. Well, except for the part when I told Micha my strange thought process about having the wedding in Star Grove because I'd feel closer to my mom. That was a little weird. But Micha being...well, Micha, he made me feel okay about feeling that way. Lighter. Which is good, because there's a chance that after I tell my dad, not just about the wedding but about my grandmother and the box she sent me, the lightness may shift to graveness.

Micha goes over to my house with me, our fingers entwined like we're kids about to tell something really bad to our parents. But we're not kids and getting married isn't a bad thing, but sometimes talking to my dad can turn that way. Although it hasn't in a while. He's actually been really nice and chatty lately.

When I enter the house, I nearly drop dead on

the floor because it's clean. There are no alcohol bottles littering the yellow and brown countertops. He's bought a new kitchen table, too, a new-used kitchen table anyway. It's white and has a bench on one side and two chairs on the other. The floor is still stained, but it has recently been swept and mopped, the air smelling like Pine-Sol mixed with cinnamon. There aren't any past-due envelopes on the counters or table. I remember the last time I was here how the house was going to get foreclosed but he managed to get it out of it, working overtime and paying the amount past due.

"Wow," Micha says as he turns in a circle, rubbing his jawline as he examines the kitchen. "I feel like I've entered an episode of *The Twilight Zone*."

I let go of his hand and cross the kitchen to the table, picking up a decorative ceramic rooster. The head pops off and it starts to make a loud rooster noise as I glance inside. "Oh my God, there's homemade cookies in it."

Micha laughs as he strolls up behind me. "You sound so adorable." He sweeps my hair to the side and his lips caress the back of my neck. "Getting excited over cookies."

I take a cookie out, put the rooster head back on, and then set it back down on the table. "So what? The only cookies I ever had when I was growing up were Oreo cookies." I bite down on the homemade chocolate chip cookie and turn around to face him. "And you would always make us share those and then would take the half with all the filling. You always gave me whatever I wanted except when it came to those damn cookies."

He steals a big bite of my cookie. "What can I say? I may love you but I love frosting just a little bit more." He swallows the cookie and then opens his mouth to steal another bite but I stuff the entire cookie into my mouth, lifting my eyebrows, giving him an arrogant look.

Arrogance rises on his face too and then he covers my mouth with his, slipping his tongue between my lips, trying to steal bites of chewed-up cookie.

I jerk back, laughing, and making a repulsed face. "You are so gross," I say, wiping my mouth with the back of my hand.

He licks his lips and then grins. "I win."

I stick out my tongue, which has gooey chewed-up cookie on it. "That is what you just ate."

His tongue slips out over his lips again. "And it was so, so good."

I shake my head, but can't stop smiling, and then I roll my eyes at myself because I'm turning into one

of those girls who gushes around their boyfriend…
fiancé…soon-to-be husband. Reality suddenly slaps
me in the face and my eyes widen.

"Holy shit, I'm going to be Ella May Scott." I breathe,
not sure whether I'm panicking or just surprised.

Micha's mouth sinks to a frown, the arrogance dissipating. I'm not sure if it's because he just realized that
too or because of my alarmed statement. I open my
mouth to say something, but then my dad enters the
kitchen and my words get stuck in my mouth.

Despite the clean sight of the kitchen, my dad still
looks grungy and rough around the edges. He's wearing an oversized plaid jacket over a holey navy-blue
shirt and his jeans have paint on them, along with the
boots he's wearing because he works as a painting
contractor now. His face is unshaven and he looks a
little heavier than the last time I saw him a year ago but
his eyes are clear, not bloodshot, and while he does
smell like cigarette smoke, it's not mixed with the smell
of booze.

He stumbles over his boots when he sees me standing in front of the table and then catches himself on the
door frame. "Holy shit." He takes a good look at me
as he blinks. "What are you doing here? I thought you
couldn't make it home this year for Christmas?"

I huddle closer to Micha, almost as a defense

mechanism. Even though I know my dad is doing much better, I can't entirely forget the past. When he was drunk. When he blamed me for my mother's death. When he wouldn't even look at me because it hurt him too much.

"Yeah, we had a change of plans," I tell him as I feel Micha's fingers brush my own.

My dad lets go of the door frame and steps up beside the counter. "Well, I'm glad, Ella," he says awkwardly, a trait that is very common whenever we're around each other. He massages the back of his neck tensely, glancing around the clean kitchen. "If I would have known you were coming, I'd have stocked up the cupboards and stuff with food or something."

"It's fine," I say. "We're actually staying over at Micha's house anyway."

My dad's gaze flickers back and forth between Micha and me. "Well, that's good, I guess."

Silence draws out between us and I can't help but think about what my mom said in the journal about him. How she wasn't thrilled to be marrying him. How her mother didn't want her to marry him. How depressed she was. Did he know about all this? Because he once told me things weren't always bad, that things used to be good between them. Was it because my mom hid her depression and dark thoughts from him?

Is that how I am with Micha since I can't seem to talk to him about my fears of getting married and having a future?

Finally Micha clears his throat and jabs me in the side with his elbow.

"Oh yeah." I shake my thoughts out of my head. "I actually have something to tell you."

My dad looks bewildered as he leans against the counter and folds his arms. "Okay."

"You remember how I told you a couple of weeks ago that Micha and I were getting married?" I rub my finger along the stones of the ring, trying to calm the nervousness in my voice. I don't even know why I'm nervous, other than that I'm worried that my dad is going to say or do something that will ruin the amazingness I've been feeling lately. I think it's just scars from my past that are causing the worry, but they're still there.

My dad nods. "Yeah, I remember."

"Well, we were going to get married in San Diego, but we decided to come back and have the wedding here," I tell him. "This weekend actually, on Christmas day."

His eyes enlarge and then travel down to my stomach. "Ella, you're not…" He shoots Micha a dirty look as he stands up straight and looks around the kitchen, avoiding eye contact with both of us, appearing uneasy even for him. "You're not…"

As it clicks what he thinks I throw my hand over my stomach. "What? No. I'm not…I'm not pregnant. God." I can't believe he'd think that. I've been careful not to let that happen and have been on the pill for a year now.

He frowns, looking unconvinced. "Okay."

Micha chuckles under his breath and I narrow my eyes at him. "This isn't funny," I hiss, but laughter threatens its way up my throat, too. I know it's not funny, especially since I found out that my mom and he got married because she was pregnant with Dean, yet it is. He's acting like a dad and it's hilarious because I'm twenty years old and this is the first real time I've seen him come even remotely close to playing the part.

"I promise she's not pregnant, Mr. Daniels," Micha says, shooting me a quick grin. "We just decided it was time."

Mr. Daniels? I mouth at him. *Really?*

Micha nonchalantly shrugs and gives me an innocent look, mouthing, *What?*

My dad's gazes flicks back and forth between Micha and me. "But you're…you're so young."

"So were you and…mom," I point out with hesitancy because it goes against what I'm trying to prove, but he doesn't know that I know about mom being pregnant when they said "I do."

"Yeah, but…" My dad trails off, staring at the back door. "That was different, though…things between your mom and me…they were complicated."

"Because she was pregnant." I reveal that I know the truth, unable to keep it in any longer. When his eyes snap wide, I add, "Mom's mom…my grandmother sent me a box of her stuff and it had this…Mom's journal in it."

There's a pause where I can hear everyone breathing and a car revs its engine from somewhere outside.

"That wasn't from your grandmother," my dad says with a heavy sigh, unfolding his arms. "Well, it was, but she didn't mail it to you. Her lawyer did."

"Her lawyer?" Micha and I say at the same time.

My dad nods, looking very uneasy. "She actually passed away about a month ago and I guess there was this box found in the nursing home with your name on it. The lawyer handling her will called me up, looking for you so he could send it to you."

She's *dead*? I'm a little shocked and I feel strangely saddened, which is weird because I never spoke to the woman. But, still, she was my grandmother.

I don't know how to react because I didn't know the woman at all, yet it makes me sort of sad, knowing I'll never get to know her. I'd even considered it for a brief second, when I'd read over her note in the box, and now the possibility is gone.

"Why didn't you give me a heads up?" I ask my dad and Micha protectively scoots closer to me, like he can sense something bad is about to happen.

My dad reaches for his cigarettes in his jacket pocket. "Because it's hard to talk to you about that stuff...especially about stuff like death and certain people."

"About my grandma?"

"And about your mother...because it was a box of her stuff and I wasn't sure how you'd react or how I felt...feel about it."

My mouth makes an *O* as my dad opens the pack, plucks out a cigarette, and plops it into his mouth. He pats down his jeans for the lighter and finds it in his back pocket. Once he gets the cigarette lit and inhales a soothing cloud of smoke, he looks more relaxed.

"It's a touchy subject for both of us." He reaches across the counter for an ashtray near the sink. He taps the cigarette on the side and then holds it in his fingers, smoke filtering through the room and erasing the delicious cinnamon scent. "But my...therapist says

I should start working on talking about it more, especially with you."

"You're seeing a therapist?" I'm surprised. "Since when?"

He looks over at Micha with reluctance, then sticks the end of the cigarette into his mouth and takes another drag. "For a month. My sponsor thought it'd be a good idea." His phone rings from inside his pocket and he holds up his finger. "Just a second," he says as he retrieves his phone. He checks the screen and then answers it, walking out of the kitchen.

"God, are all the Danielses seriously messed up?" I mutter under my breath. "He's seeing a therapist, too? First my brother, then me, and now my dad. It could be like the family motto: enter my family and your head's going to get messed up and you'll have to have a shrink put it back together again." I peek over at Micha.

"Don't even think it," he warns. "You're not crazy and you're not going to ruin my life. You'll only ruin it if you leave me."

His words remind me that I'm not that person anymore, the one who pushes people away. *I need him and he needs me.* "I'm not going anywhere. I promise." I blow out a breath. "But can you give me a minute?" I ask him. "I think I need to talk to my dad alone."

He seems reluctant. "Are you sure? Because I don't

mind hanging around even if it means enduring your dad's awkwardness."

I nod and give his hand a comforting squeeze. "I just want to ask him a few things about my mom and I think he'll answer more easily if it's just me."

Micha remains still for a few seconds longer and then, nodding, he backs away, holding onto my hand until we're far enough away that our fingers slip apart. "If you're not back in, like, an hour," he says, opening the back door and letting snow and a chilly breeze gust in, "then I'm coming back for you."

"Micha, what do you think's going to happen?" I joke. "It's just my dad."

He intensely holds my gaze, making a point without saying it. There have been many times where painful, hurtful things have happened between my dad and me.

"All right, see you in an hour," I promise and he steps outside, drawing his hood over his head as he shuts the door.

I pull out a chair and sink down into it, then steal another cookie from the rooster jar. I'm stuffing the last bit of it into my mouth when my dad walks in, clutching his phone.

He glances around the empty chairs. "Where'd Micha go?"

I swallow the cookie and brush the crumbs off the

table. "Home for a little bit, so you and I could talk about some stuff."

"Yeah, we do need to talk." He sits down, then glances at the rooster on the table without the lid on. "I see you found the cookies."

"Yeah, but who made them?" I wonder curiously. "You?"

He shakes his head as he puts the lid back on. "No, Amanda did."

"Who's Amanda?"

"This woman I met while I was staying at the alcoholism treatment center."

"Was she another recovering alcoholic?" I ask.

"No." He pushes his sleeves up and rests his arms on the table. "She was the secretary there."

"Oh," I say. "So...are you, like, dating her?"

He scratches his head. "Um...sort of...I guess."

"Oh," I say, at a loss for words. It's weird he's dating because he's my dad and the only person I've seen him with is my mom, but then again their relationship was beyond rocky. "Is she the one who cleaned the house?"

His hand falls from his head to the table. "No, I cleaned it. Why?"

I shrug. "Just wondered. It looks nice."

He gives me a look, like he wants to say more, but

then he changes the subject, relaxing back in the chair. "So what was in the box?" he asks rigidly. "I know it was stuff that belonged to your mother, but what exactly?"

"Mom's journal and a few other things, like drawings and photos." I pause at the sudden increase of my heart rate. "I didn't know she liked to draw."

He stares down at the table with a sad look on his face. "She did when she was younger," he says quietly. "But she stopped not too long after we got married."

It's so hard to talk about this aloud, asking him questions, but I force myself to continue because I want to know—understand. "Why did she stop?"

When he glances up, his eyes are little watery. "Because she stopped enjoying it and so there was no point, at least that's what she told me."

I trace the patterns of the wood in the table, staring down at them, because I can't look him in the eye with what I'm about to say. "You told me once, when I was...when I was dropping you off at the recovery clinic, that things weren't always bad. But when was that? I know her bipolar disorder progressively got worse, but even from the start it always felt like Mom was sad all the time."

He's silent for a while and I worry I might have

upset him. But when I look up at him, he's just staring at me like I'm a person, not a painful reminder of the woman he once loved, which is how he used to look at me all the time.

"Things were never one hundred percent normal when it came to your mom," he says, his voice strained. "But in the beginning she had way more ups than she did downs. And her...episodes...they were few and far between."

"Was she ever happy?"

Again it takes him a moment to answer. "She was happy sometimes. I think anyway. It was so hard to tell."

"Why was it so hard to tell?" Deep down, though, I think I know the answer. Because sometimes it's hard to be happy or to even admit that you're good enough to be happy, that you do deserve it, so you refuse to feel it, fight it. It's my own thought process sometimes and I hate it, but I've also learned to deal with it...I think.

He smiles, but it's a sad smile. "It's just the way she was, Ella May. And I really want to believe she was happy, even though she didn't show it."

It's weird hearing him call me that and it throws me off and I let a question slip out that I probably shouldn't. "Why did you love her?" I ask and then pull a remorseful face. "I'm sorry, Dad. You don't have to answer that."

He shakes his head, more water building up in his eyes. "It's okay. You can ask me things. I'm doing better with...stuff." He pauses, deliberating, and then his breath falters. "I loved her because in the beginning she was erratic and impulsive and she could make life really surprising and...unpredictable. " He stares over my shoulder, lost in memories and for a brief moment he almost looks happy. Then he blinks his eyes several times and the look disappears before he turns his attention back to me. "I think she was happy when she had you. And Dean."

I can't tell if he's lying, but I don't really care if he is or not. He might just be saying it to make me happy and I'll take it. "Thanks, Dad."

"No problem." He seems like he wants to say more, squirming and popping his neck, like he has nervous energy flowing through him. "Ella, I don't want to make you mad but I...I really wish you'd think about waiting to get married."

What? "Why?"

"Because..." He rubs the back of his neck and leaves his hand there with his elbow bent upward.

"You're so young...and should live your life before you tie yourself down to grown-up stuff." He lets his arm fall to his side.

It takes me a moment to speak, because there are a lot of mean words that want to push their way up my throat. Like the fact that I was tied down by grown-up stuff since I was four. Bills. Cooking. Cleaning. Taking care of people. That stuff is not new to me.

"I'll think about it," I say, but I don't mean it. I back toward the door, zipping my jacket up. "And, Dad... thanks for talking about Mom."

"No problem," he replies. "I should have talked about her more, I guess."

I don't say anything. I agree with him, but I don't want to say it because it'll only hurt him, ruin this whole weird, good father/daughter vibe we have going. I open the back door and the wind blows inside, dusting snow across the floor.

"And, Ella," he calls out as I'm about to step out into the snow and the glacier-cold breeze.

I pause and glance over my shoulder. "Yeah?"

"If you need any help...I mean, with the wedding and stuff if you decide to do it...I'm here if you need me," he says, shifting his weight.

"Thanks," I tell him, confused because he wants to help and it's not something I'm used to. "I'll let you know, but I think Micha's mom's on top of a lot of stuff. She's super excited."

He looks a little bit disappointed and I open my mouth to say more, but I can't think of anything else to say so I wave, walk outside, and shut the door behind me. I feel somewhat bad because he seemed upset about my declining his help, but at the end of the day Micha's mom was more of a parent to me than either of mine. She and Micha were my family since I was four, not my dad, my mom, or Dean. It was just his mom and Micha, but mainly Micha. He was my past and he is my future.

I pause as I'm about to hop over the fence, the snow knee-deep and soaking through my jeans as I have a revelation that slams me square in the chest. From the day Micha begged me to climb over the fence for the very first time, we've been inseparable, except for the time I ran away to college. He took care of me. He loved me. He showed me what love was. And I think deep down, even though I couldn't admit it a couple of years ago, I secretly hoped that he'd be in my life forever—that I'd end up with him. That I'd still be hopping over the fence to see him when I was twenty years old with his ring on my finger. That fifty years down the road I'd still be with him, sitting on a porch swing, drinking lemonade or whatever it is old couples do.

It makes my heart thump in excitement and terror because I think it's time to let go of the dark things that haunt my past, let things go that I might not want to, so I can move forward into a future with a simple fence, juice box, and a toy car.

Chapter Fourteen

Micha

"Are you sure you want me to do this?" I ask Ella, staring down at her mother's journal on my lap.

She nods as she digs through her bag on the floor. "Yeah, I only want to know if you find anything happy." She peers up at me, wearing only a red-and-black bra and matching panties. "If you don't, then I don't need to read it. But if you do, then I want to read it just so I can hear about the happy part of her I never got to see."

I massage the back of my neck, nervous about reading something so private. "Okay, if that's what you want."

"It is." She straightens her legs and stands up with a black dress in her hand. "But only if you feel comfortable doing it."

I want to say that I'm not but there's no way that

161

I'm going to. Not after she came into the house yesterday after talking to her dad and announced that she was ready to move forward without finishing the journal because she wanted to let go of the past. I'm not even sure where the declaration came from, but there's no way I'm going to do anything that will ruin it. "I'm down for a little reading, I guess." I move the journal off my lap and onto the bed, then lean forward and grab the edge of the short, tight dress she's about to put on. "Just as long as you tell me where the hell you're going wearing this?"

"Out to dinner with Lila," she answers. "Why? What's wrong with the dress?"

"Because it's smaller than most of my shirts," I tell her, jealousy ringing in my voice. "Your ass will be hanging out of it."

She snatches the dress away from me. "It will not," she insists, bending over and stepping into the dress. "Besides, Lila said specifically to wear this one."

I rise to my feet as she shimmies the tight fabric over her body and slips her arms through the thin straps. It hugs her body perfectly but the bottom barely covers her thighs. "Why?" I question.

She tousles her fingers through her hair. "I'm not sure. You'll have to ask her. All she'd tell me was that it was a surprise."

"Oh, I'm going to," I assure her and then leave the room to go find Lila.

She's in the kitchen with Ethan, bags of red and black candles and matching flowers, ribbons, and other decorative shit scattered all over the countertops and table in front of them, along with wrapping paper and tape and a bag full of Christmas present bows. Lila, Ella, and my mom spent half the day shopping and Ella had come home looking worn out but with a bag full of wedding decorations and I guess a few presents for Christmas. She never was the shopping type and I'm guessing that Lila and my mom had more to do with the overabundance of wedding decorations and presents than Ella.

"I have a question for you," I say to Lila as I scoot out a chair and join them at the table. She's got Ethan tying ribbons, and even though he doesn't look happy, he's still doing it, which is kind of funny.

"Don't say a word," Ethan warns as he ties a piece of black ribbon into a bow. "Time and time again I've watched you do stupid shit for Ella and haven't said a word."

I rotate a candle in my hand. "No, you said a lot of words that annoyed the shit out of me."

He shakes his head and then drops the bow, looking at Lila. "Can I be done with this?" He flexes his fingers like he has a cramp. "I can't even feel the tips of my fingers anymore."

Lila snips the end of a red piece of ribbon with a pair of scissors. "No way. We have about a hundred more to go." She sets the ribbon and scissors down. She's wearing this dark blue dress that has sparkly stuff all over it. It's not as tight as Ella's but it is equally short, if not shorter. "So what's your question, Micha? And if it's about your Christmas present from Ella, I'm not going to tell you what it is."

"It's not that," I say, shaking my head. "And what are you talking about? Ella and I don't get each other presents." Except for last year when I gave her the engagement ring, but that was different.

"Maybe not in the past," she says with a smile. "But she did this year."

Shit. Does that mean I have to get her something? And if so, then what? I shake my head. I'm getting sidetracked. I shove the candle aside and fold my arms on top of the table. "That's not what I was going to ask you. I want to know where the hell you're taking Ella tonight."

Lila shrugs as she reaches for another roll of ribbon. "Out to dinner."

"Where?" I ask.

"Why does it matter?" she replies, unraveling a bit of ribbon around her hand.

"Because she's dressed like a whore," I say bluntly, attempting to throw her off.

But it doesn't faze her. "She isn't going to look like a whore. She's just dressing up to go out."

"Not to dinner, though. You don't need to be dressed like that to go to dinner," I say and point at her dress.

"What's wrong with how I'm dressed?" She bats her eyelashes innocently. "I'm just wearing a dress."

"I'm going to agree with Micha on this one," Ethan chimes in, cracking his knuckles. "I don't like the dress at all."

Amusement dances in Lila's eyes. "You liked it the other night."

"Yeah, when I was the only one seeing you in it," he says, extending his hand toward the heap of ribbon Lila unraveled.

Lila grins as she pushes her chair away from the table. "Oh, you two and your jealousy." She pats Ethan on the top of the head. "It's so adorable." She strolls behind him and kisses the top of his head. "I'm going to go see if Ella's ready," she singsongs and Ethan checks her ass out as she walks away and leaves the room, calling over her shoulder, "And Micha, feel free to make yourself useful and start tying bows."

I gape at Ethan. "Is she being serious?"

He cuts a piece of red ribbon. "Yeah." He drops the scissors onto the table. "But it's your fault."

"Why the hell is it my fault?"

"Because you're the one who wouldn't just drive to Vegas and elope."

I reach over the table and pick up a roll of ribbon. "That sounds more like your kind of marriage than mine."

He nods in agreement. "Yeah, you're right, still though. We wouldn't have to be sitting here, tying ribbon like a couple of whipped pussies."

I fiddle with the ribbon, stifling a laugh. "So what am I supposed to be doing?"

Sighing, he shows me how to tie the ribbon and then we sit at the table tying bows for the next twenty minutes until Ella and Lila walk into the kitchen. Ella stops just short of the table and crosses her arms. Her hair is loose at her shoulders in waves, her eyes are lined with black, and her lips have a tint of pink to them. She has heels on that have straps that wind up her ankles, and between the shoes and the short dress her legs look nearly endless.

"Well, look at you two," she says with hilarity in her voice. "All crafty and tying bows."

I rotate in the chair and scan her amazingly perfect body, picturing how later her long legs will be wrapped around me. "You better watch it, Ella May, or you won't have any ribbons at your wedding."

"Good," she says, tugging the bottom of her dress down.

Lila pokes her in the back. "Hey, I thought you liked the ribbons."

Ella pulls an apologetic face. "No, I said out of all the silly, frilly decoration stuff you guys were throwing at me, the red and black ribbons were the least annoying."

Lila frowns disappointedly. "So you don't like it?"

Ella sighs. "No, I do. Sorry, I'm not being very nice right now. You're helping me and I should be more grateful."

Now Lila sighs. "Don't lie to me. If you don't like the ribbons then you don't. We can do something else."

Ethan shoots me a funny look and then reclines back in the chair with his arm draped over the top of it. "You know, if I didn't know any better I'd think it was you two who were getting married."

Lila's heels click against the floor as she strolls over and gives him a kiss on the cheek. "All right, it's time for you to get back to your bow tying," she says as she walks toward the back door and Ella follows her.

As Ella's passing by me, I snag her elbow and pull her back, drawing her down so her head lowers and then I put my lips beside her ear. "Don't get into any trouble, please."

She tilts her head to look at me. "When have I ever gotten into any trouble?"

"If you want me to ramble off the list," I reply, "then I will, but it'll probably take the rest of the night."

She attempts to restrain a smile as she scowls at me, but then it slips through and she kisses me deeply. "I'll do my best not to get into any fights," she says, backing away, a little breathless from the kiss. "Or any other trouble."

"And try not to wreck my car," I call out as Lila opens the door.

"You're letting them take your car?" Ethan asks, looking at me like I'm insane.

I shrug. "What else are they going to drive?"

"They'd be better off walking," he mutters, and then yells out to Lila and Ella, "Don't drive drunk or shove any dollar bills down dudes' pants."

"We're not going to a strip club," Lila retorts, but then giggles as she retrieves her jacket from the coat rack.

Ella puts on her leather jacket, covering up a little bit and making me feel slightly better about the dress. She opens her mouth to say something but Lila snatches her arm and yanks her outside, slamming the door. Thomas and my mom went out for dinner and the house is really quiet as Ethan and I sit in silence, taking in what just happened.

"Do you kind of feel like their bitches?" he asks, turning around in the chair with ribbon in his hand.

I stare at the pile of ribbon and candles on the table. "Yeah, kind of."

We exchange a look and then simultaneously push away from the table and get to our feet.

"So the question is," Ethan says as he grabs his jacket off the back of the chair, "do we want to go to a bar or go somewhere noisy, like a party?"

"We could always follow them," I joke as I walk over to the coat rack beside the back door. "Play creepy stalkers for the night." I grab my jacket and slip it on, pretending like I'm joking but deep down I'm serious. I don't like the idea of Ella going out dressed like that, in this town. Not only is she too beautiful and sexy for her own good, but she's also got history in this town, with people who either overly like her or with people who loathe her. And if the feisty Ella makes a grand appearance, especially the drunk one, a lot of shit could happen.

"That's not a bad idea," Ethan agrees, responding to my joke, looking serious. "But we don't have a car."

"Should we just start walking?" I ask as I open the door.

It's late, the black sky is clear of clouds and the stars are shining. Lights twinkle from next door and reflect off the ice covering the yard.

Ethan zips up his jacket. "Sure."

We step outside and hike down the driveway through the snow, then make a left toward town. The snow on the sidewalk crunches under our boots and our breath fogs out in front of us. It's freezing, but it's not the first time we've walked around late at night in below-zero temperatures.

"So I'm waiting for you to panic," Ethan unexpectedly announces, kicking a chunk of ice out of the way.

I stuff my hands into my jacket pockets. "Panic over what?"

"Over getting married."

"Why would I panic?"

He gapes at me. "Because you're going to be with one person for the rest of your life, and that the rest of your life decisions are going to be based on what's best for not just you but for you and her. You can't just do whatever you want anymore."

"Have I ever really been with anyone else though?" I ask. "I mean relationship-wise."

He shrugs. "No, I guess not, but still. It's such a huge responsibility and there seems like there should be a little panic involved, even if it's for a minute."

"Not really," I say. "At least if it's the right person."

He takes in my words with a perplexed look as he stares at the ground. Finally he shakes his head and then looks up. "And what happens if Ella tells you that she doesn't want you going on that Slam Tour or whatever?"

"Then I won't go," I say. I told Ethan about my dilemma the other day, while we were cleaning up the house the morning after the party, because I needed to get it off my chest.

"You'd just give up your dream?" he asks.

I nod. "Yeah, pretty much."

"And what happens, like, five years down the road when you look back and regret it?"

I kick the tip of my boot at the snow. "Why are you pushing this so hard? I mean, I know you're not a fan of Ella, but it's like you're trying to talk me out of marrying her, which will never happen."

He abruptly halts near the edge of the curb and I slip on the ice as I slam to a stop beside him. My hands go out to my sides and I quickly regain my balance.

"I'm not telling you not to marry her," he says with a frown. "I'm just telling you that since you're going to marry her, you need to talk to her about the tour and make the decision together about whether or not you're going to go. Otherwise you're going to get married in a few days without talking about something major and that could lead to problems."

"You're so weird sometimes," I tell him, pulling my hood over my head. "You give relationship advice all the time, yet I've never seen you in a relationship except for with Lila, but somehow your advice makes sense."

He shrugs, staring at the single-story brick home across the street that is covered in flashing red and green lights. "I watched my parents do the wrong things for years and years, so I know what doesn't work," he says as we cross the street. "Now, whether or not my advice is the right way to go, I really have no idea."

I hop up onto the curb, stuffing my hands back into my jacket pockets. "I'll talk to her tomorrow."

He doesn't say anything, but I can tell he's glad I said I would, for whatever reason. "You know what?" he says, changing the subject. "I think we need to have a bachelor party tonight. It seems wrong that we're not having a real one."

"Yeah, I think you're forgetting what the strip bars look like around here," I say to him unenthusiastically. "Remember when we decided to go to one right after we graduated?" I shudder at the thought. "I think I'm still a little scarred over the things I saw."

His face contorts in revulsion. "Yeah, how could I

forget?" As we round the corner of the street, heading east, he adds, "But we could go get drunk, just for old times' sake." He sticks out his fist. "What do you say? You want to get trashed down at the pub one more time?"

I pound fists with him. We haven't hung out in a while, ever since I moved, so I don't get many chances to hang out with him. "Yeah, why the hell not? One last time, for old times' sake."

I can't help but smile at the many times Ethan and I snuck into the pub with our fake IDs. We always had a lot of fun and it hits me that we've sort of moved on from that stuff. It's kind of sad, but at the same time, I'm glad we've moved on from this town, moved forward in our lives, because not a lot of people around here do.

Chapter Fifteen

Ella

"I can't believe you brought me here," I shout over the chest-bumping music, fanning my hand in front of my face because it's hot and smells like sweat and old cheese mixed with beer. There are strings of Christmas lights coiling around the ceiling beams and they sparkle across our faces, giving our skin a pink glow.

Lila pivots in her stool, her eyes skimming the dance floor. "Well, I asked around and everyone said this was the place to go to have a little fun."

I shake my head as I pick up my drink. "Oh, Lila Dila, fun in Star Grove is not the same as California fun or even Vegas fun." I rotate in the stool, motioning my hand at the crowd of rough-looking people, most dressed in old jeans, plaid shirts, T-shirts, boots. We aren't the only ones dressed up, but girls wearing fancy dresses are few and far between. And there's no flashy lights or décor, just low lighting due to a few lightbulbs being out, round tables and mismatched chairs, and peanut shells and wrappers on the floor. The music is coming from a stereo, not a DJ, but the good thing is the drinks are cheap.

"Well, I wanted to give you one last hoorah before you tie the knot in a few days," she says, sipping on the straw that's in her margarita as the bartender, a middle-aged guy with thinning hair and a mustache, eyes us down. He's been doing it since we walked in, checking us out, but so far it's been easy to ignore him. "I was trying to be a good maid of honor."

"Didn't we already do that back in San Diego the night before the wedding?" I ask. "When you took me out for drinks at that club?"

She raises her eyebrows at me. "The wedding that never happened?"

"True," I say. "But we still had our hoorah."

She slurps the rest of her drink before reclining back in the stool and setting it on the counter. "You can never have too many last hoorahs." She frowns as she sits up straight. "We've barely seen each other in the last six months and now we're hardly going to see each other anymore after you get married."

I'm not the heart-to-heart kind of girl but she's

making me feel bad. "Lila, we'll still be friends no matter what. And you're dating Micha's best friend. We'll see each other more than you think."

She rearranges a few strands of her hair back into place. "No, we won't. You'll see. You'll move on, probably have babies, and I'll still be living in Vegas, trying to figure out what I want to do with my life."

"That's not what I hear," I tell her. "I heard that you and Ethan have a big road trip planned."

She seals her lips as she watches the dance floor. "Yeah, I guess that's the plan."

"Then why do you sound so unconvinced?"

"I don't know. Shit happens, you know. Things sometimes change."

I take another swallow of my drink. "Is there something going on between you and Ethan? Are you fighting or something?"

She shakes her head. "No, but it doesn't mean that I don't worry about all the things that can go wrong."

"Like what?"

"Like life." She turns toward me, crossing her legs. "Not all of us have the perfect relationship, although I can't say that what Ethan and I have is bad. It's great, but it's not like I have a ring on my finger."

"Yet," I say, and she rolls her eyes at me. I throw my head back and guzzle the rest of my drink, feeling the burn of the vodka as it slides down my throat. "Besides, I don't have the perfect relationship." I put the glass on the bar. "Need I remind you I stood Micha up just a few days ago."

"Yeah, but you had a reason; right? Because you were worried about your future." The way she says it with suspicion makes me wonder if she doesn't believe my reasoning.

"Yeah," I say. "And because of other stuff...things I don't like to talk about."

"What kind of stuff? Is there something else you're not telling me?"

I twirl a strand of my hair around my finger, feeling uncomfortable. I can tell Micha personal things about me but he's my best friend, fiancé, my everything, which sounds so cheesy but it's true. *I wonder if I should put it in the vows.*

The burn of the alcohol rushes through my veins and I begin to think maybe it's time to talk to Lila about stuff. She's usually good about giving advice and maybe she can direct me on what to do. But I don't want to talk about my mom and the box—I talked enough about that with my dad. But there is something else.

"I'm having trouble writing my vows," I admit.

She props her elbow on the countertop as her eyebrows knit. "You guys are writing vows?"

I nod. "It was Micha's idea."

Lila drums her fingernails on her knee. "Yeah, I assumed as much." She pauses. "Why do you think you're having such a hard time?"

"Because I'm not a writer," I say. "And because... well, because I hate expressing my emotions to an empty room, let alone to people."

"Yeah, but we already kind of know how you feel about Micha, since you can't keep your hands off him." She inspects her reflection in the mirror on the back wall of the bar. "But I get the emotion part and not wanting to say it to anyone. Sometimes I hide what I feel, too."

"Really?" I ask, raising my voice as the music gets louder. "It never seems like you do."

She glares at some creepy guy with a ponytail who keeps grinning at her from across the bar. "Maybe it's not that I hide what I'm feeling so much as I pretend to feel something else, but I've been trying to stop because it's unhealthy."

I know from experience that she's right. "So how do you suggest I get over the not being a writer part?"

"You just put the pen to the paper and write, I guess." She shrugs. "I'm sure something good will come out."

I continue to try to figure out a better solution until

the song switches to an upbeat tempo and Lila claps her hands together, her eyes lighting up with excitement. "I love this song," she says. "Let's take another shot and dance."

"I'm only taking a shot if it's Jäger," I tell her.

She makes a gagging face. "Ew, you're so gross. I'll just stick with tequila."

She orders our drinks, and then we slam them back and head for the dance floor. We dance in the low lighting, making the occasional trip back to the bar for more shots until we're hot, sweaty, exhausted, and ready to go home. I feel good, not just because I'm buzzed, but because I had fun, even though I'm scared of getting married, worried about writing vows.

As we push through the crowd, heading for the exit, we collect our jackets from the chair. We slip them on as we push out the door and the ice-cold air makes my bare legs sting.

"Let's run," I tell Lila and she laughs as we take off, staggering and slipping in the ice as we run toward the Chevelle parked beneath the lamppost.

"Wait." Lila suddenly slams to a stop when we're almost to the car. She looks back at the club with a torn expression on her face. "Maybe we should go back inside where it's warm and call the guys to come get us. We said we wouldn't drive drunk."

Through the sea of alcohol sloshing around in my head, I realize that we indeed shouldn't be driving since everything looks a little distorted and standing seems complex. "Yeah, good idea." I start to turn around to head back when a blue Camaro drives into the parking lot and parks between us and the door to the club, blocking our path.

"You have got to be shitting me," I mutter as the window rolls down.

Mikey sticks his head out as a cloud of smoke rushes from the open window. The last time I saw him I was throwing a milkshake into his window and then he tried to chase us down. Knowing Mikey, I'm guessing he's probably still holding a grudge.

"Ella, what's wrong?" Lila asks tracking my line of sight as a smile creeps up Mikey's face. "Who is that?"

"Well, well, if it isn't the town rebel." He continues smiling as he opens his door and hops out. He's about average height for a guy, which makes me in heels as tall as him, but my weight is no match for his. His black hair blends with the night, his nose is crooked, probably because someone clocked him, and he has a barbed-wire tattoo curving around his neck.

His boots stomp against the icy parking lot as he strides over to us with a smirk on his face. "So is that

Gregory idiot with you, because I've been dying to kick his ass too for that shake stunt you two pulled."

"What?" Lila asks way too loud and I shoot her a look over my shoulder, warning her to keep her mouth shut. Then I glance over at Mikey's car, noting that there's someone else in the passenger seat, a guy, I think.

As Mikey slows to a stop in front of us, he measures Lila up with a sly look on his face. "Are you his girl or something?"

"Whose girl?" Lila plays dumb, shielding herself by stepping behind me. She's scared, her erratic breathing showing through the fog.

Mikey looks her over for a little bit longer and then focuses on me. I don't like how he's looking at me, not like I'm Ella the girl who could hang tight with the guys, even if he didn't like me. He's looking at me like I'm a girl, because I'm dressed like one and I suddenly regret wearing the damn dress and fucking heels. "Ella, I know you're not stupid," he says, inching closer. "I know you know that around here people just don't get away with throwing shakes in cars. They have to pay—things have to be even."

I roll my eyes and cross my arms over my chest. "Just like I know that no one around here respects you."

The muscles in his neck tighten as he steps into the

light from the lamppost. I'm growing a little nervous. Even though Mikey has always tried to seem tough, it was all an act and most of us knew that he was a lot of talk. But this Mikey looks different than the one I used to know. More ragged, rough, intense, and less cowardly. His eyes are sunken in and red and I wonder if he's gotten into drugs, but it doesn't really surprise me if he has. It happens sometimes in this town.

"Watch your fucking mouth," Mikey cautions.

Lila captures my arm, her fingers trembling as she whispers, "Maybe I should call or text Micha and Ethan."

I shake my head and hiss, "No way. Then they'll just end up in a fight."

Lila glances at Mikey. "I think we might end up in a fight if we don't get them here," she whispers nervously.

"No, we're fine," I reassure her, even though I'm not so sure myself. "Just go to the car and wait for me." I turn around and target my eyes on Mikey, attempting to look tougher than I feel as Lila backs toward the Chevelle.

He cracks his knuckles and neck, like it proves he's tough. "You think you can frighten me with a look?" He spans his arms out to the side at the empty parking lot. "You got no one around to protect your ass."

That feisty, fighting girl that I keep shoved down

inside pushes her way out and I step forward so we're close. "And that's okay." I span my hands out to the side and glance around, mockingly imitating his move, ignoring the fact that I know things are going to get ugly. There's nothing I can do about it. I could run, but then he'd just chase me. "Since I don't see any threat around."

A vein bulges in his neck and he starts to pace to the side while the other guy in the car climbs out. He's tall and bulky with cropped hair and arms the size of my legs. I try to calculate how fast I can run to the car in heels, and if I make it to the car, can I drive fast enough to get away because I know he's going to chase me down whether on foot or in a vehicle.

"Ah, now you're not so cocky," Mikey says with a smirk when I don't respond. I hate to back down because it would mean living through hell for almost forever, since no one in Star Grove can seem to forget, but at the same time this isn't my home. I might be here for holidays, if that, so in the end, does it even matter?

Sucking in all of my stubbornness, I put my hands up and step back, putting distance between us. "Fine, you win," I say through gritted teeth.

"No fucking way." He counters my step back, narrowing the distance between us. "You insulted me and ruined the leather in my car. You don't just walk away.

The question is, how are you going to pay? I mean, I could just make you pay to get it reupholstered." His eyes scroll up my body suggestively. "Although, there might be something else you can give me."

I can't help it. I burst out laughing, which probably isn't the best thing to do, but I'm drunk and not thinking rationally. Big Guy starts rushing for me as I back away with my hand over my stomach, my laughter echoing around us. But he slips and eats it, falling flat on his back and I laugh harder and Mikey's face heats with anger. He snatches my arm and jerks me forward, his fingers pressing against my skin and I wince as I stumble.

"Fuck off," I say, yanking my arm back.

His fingers dig tighter as he wrenches me forward, opening his mouth to say something, but I bring my knee up and slam it in his manly parts. I'm not sure how much force is behind the blow since I'm intoxicated and having a hard time keeping my balance, but it seems to do the job and he frees me from his hold, clutching his junk as his face contorts in pain. I'm about to turn and run when he lifts his arm and strikes me across the cheek.

My ears ring and I see spots as I clutch my cheek and blink. "You fucking asshole!" I shout, pissed off. Some girls would have cried, but the pain only makes me want to get him back. I see the big guy walking toward us as Mikey lifts his hand to hit me again. I bring back my own hand and slam my fist into his cheek. It's not the first time I've hit someone and I'm pretty sure it won't be my last, but no matter how many times I punch someone in the face, it still hurts my God damn hand.

We both cry out in pain, Mikey cupping his jaw where I clocked him while I shake out my hand as I scramble away from him, ready to bolt for the car. But then a group of guys and girls exit the bar, creating a lot of noise and making it so there are now witnesses.

One of the guys sends a questioning look in our direction as he lights up a cigarette and I seize the opportunity to hurry over to the Chevelle and climb in with Lila.

Her eyes are huge and dotted with tears and her arms are wrapped around herself. "Oh my God, Ella. That was—"

"Star Grove," I tell her, then add, "Lock your door."

She obeys as I lock mine, too.

Mikey goes up to one of the guys who just walked out and they exchange a handshake while big guy stares me down with his arms folded over his chest. I reach for my phone inside my pocket, debating who to call. I know that if I call Micha he's going to come here and if Mikey's still here then there's a good chance a fight's going to go down and that's the last thing I want.

"I already called them the second that asshole came after you," Lila tells me. "They were at a pub a few blocks over. They're headed here right now."

"Shit, Lila, now they're going to come here ready to throw punches." I glance in the rearview mirror, wincing as I touch my red, puffy cheekbone. "I think it's going to bruise."

Lila frowns. "Great, now you'll have a giant bruise in all of your wedding pictures."

"What pictures?"

"The ones Caroline's going to take." She slaps her hand over her mouth. "Oh shit, I wasn't supposed to tell you that."

"What?" I gape at her as I cradle my injured hand. "Who invited them?"

She drops her hand from her mouth to her lap. "Micha's mom. She thought it would be good for you to have your brother here."

I'm not sure how to respond. My quiet wedding is now turning into a bunch of people who are going to be staring at me while I seal my future and of course read the vows I haven't even started to write. It shouldn't seem like a big deal, but at the same time it does. Especially if I do something stupid like panic. I don't want anyone to see me panic.

I slump back in the seat and keep my eyes locked on Mikey, who's still chatting with the guy. "God, I forgot how intense this town is," I say, changing the subject. "Everything is either life or death."

"Why don't I just drive somewhere close?" Lila suggests, reaching for the door handle to get out of the car and switch seats with me "I feel sober enough now to at least get us away from here and then we can tell Micha and Ethan to meet us somewhere else so they won't have to show up here and get into a fight."

"It doesn't matter where we go," I tell her. "Mikey will just chase us down. In fact, I bet he's hoping we drive somewhere just so he *can* chase us."

"What is wrong with that guy?" she asks, looking at Mikey. "He hit a girl."

"It's just how people are around here." I put the keys in the ignition, debating whether or not to start the car and turn the heat on. It's cold as death in here but at the same time the rev of the engine might set Mikey off. If my vision weren't slightly blurred I'd totally take on racing Mikey in a heartbeat, but I have a feeling that if I try anything right now, I could end up wrapping the car around a tree. Lila could get hurt, or someone else, and if something happened to me then that lovely future Micha and I have planned will be gone. The last thought sits in my chest, but in a good way because a few years ago I'd have driven the car and risked it all.

Some of the girls start off for a truck, lighting up a cigarette and passing it around, and the guys soon follow, waving at Mikey and the big guy. A gangly guy with a beanie on lingers behind and then he says something to Mikey and then all three of them climb into the Camaro.

"What are they doing?" Lila slants forward in the seat and squints at the Camaro as Mikey rolls up the window. He doesn't drive away, but he does turn the headlights off.

I thrum my fingers on top of the steering wheel. "Probably dealing drugs."

"Oh." Lila frowns and then stares out the window to the side of her. I'm about to say we should just take off on foot and meet Micha and Ethan when someone knocks on the window.

I jump but relax when I see Micha standing outside with the hood of his jacket pulled over his head and this relaxed look on his face like he's had more than beers to drink tonight. Ethan is beside him and when he glances inside the car, he winds around the front, heading toward Lila's side.

"When they ask what happened, tell them it was a

girl who hit me," I whisper to Lila and then unlock the door.

Micha backs up so I can open the door and then he ducks his head to look in the car, his blond hair hanging in his eyes. "What happened?" he asks, his breath smelling like an array of different alcohols. He carefully looks me over and then his eyes flare as he notes my swollen cheek. "How the hell did that happen?" He glances over at Lila and then his burning gaze lands back on me. "Lila said you guys needed help."

I shrug as Lila opens her door and I hear Ethan say something to her about looking so hot. "There was this bitch in the club who we used to go to school with," I tell Micha. "Apparently I kicked her ass one time and she was drunk and wanted to fight. Lila panicked and called you guys, even though I told her I could handle it."

"Hey." Lila pokes me in the back and I flinch. "You were not handling it very well."

I discreetly glance over at Mikey's Camaro that's still parked in front of the door. "I handled it fine. Can we just go home now?"

Micha crouches down, his eyebrows knitting. "Yeah, I think that might be a problem." He leans to the side and laughs this silly drunk laugh as he says to Ethan, "I think we were lucky to even make it here."

"You're drunk," I remark and Micha looks back at me with a guilty face. It's been a while since I've seen him drunk and it worries me, not because I think he's going to be mean but because if Mikey comes over and tries to start something Micha is more likely to pick a fight and more likely to lose.

"Maybe," Micha admits with an adorable grin on his face. "But I won't be mean and hurt you." He presses his hand to his heart. "I said I'd never hurt you again and I won't. In fact, I'll be really, really nice if you let me," he says, glancing at my chest. "I'll do all sorts of nice things to you…" His fingers spread across the top of my leg.

I roll my eyes while Lila and Ethan giggle over something. I don't dare turn around, worried about what I might see the two of them doing if I do.

Out of the corner of my eye, I check on Mikey's car, relieved it's still parked and quiet. "I think we should go home," I say, looking back at Micha.

"And how do you suppose we should do that?" Micha asks innocently as he glances around at the four of us, then chuckles under his breath. "Is anyone sober? Because I'm not."

"I'm not either," Ethan says with a slur to his speech and Lila laughs even louder.

I blink my eyes, hoping the blur and merry-go-round

effect has vanished, but no such luck. "No, but we could always call your mom," I say, racking my mind for more ideas, but all I get is a headache.

Micha waves me off and staggers to his feet, grinning proudly like he's just come up with the best idea ever. "Nah, we can just walk. Walking's fun."

I laugh as he tugs me to my feet and grips my waist to hold my balance as I stumble in my heels. "Easy for you to say," I tell him, gripping onto his shoulder as we both slide on the ice. "You're not the one wearing heels."

He works to steady us and then his eyes roam down my legs as he sucks his lip ring in between his teeth. "God, those are some fucking sexy legs." His eyes heat with lust and I know if I don't get him home soon, I'm going to have my hands even fuller. If a fight doesn't break out, then a live porn show might. "I just want to rub my hands all over them," he growls, moving in for a kiss.

I laugh louder, trying not to trip as I gently put my hand to his chest and push him back. "I'll tell you what, you call your mom to come get us and I'll let you rub my legs as long as you want."

"Promise?" he asks, with an intense look on his face.

I cross my heart with my finger. "Promise, but make

sure she brings Thomas. We can't leave your car here." Otherwise it'll probably get trashed.

He grins at me and then retrieves his phone out of his pocket to call his mom. I keep an eye on Mikey's car, hoping he stays in there until we're gone, because if he gets out and Micha finds out he hit me, all shit's going to hit the fan. Micha isn't the most violent person, except when it comes to me. I remember how Micha told me he punched Grantford Davis because he was the one who drove me to the bridge that night.

"Okay, she'll be here in, like, five," Micha announces, stuffing his phone back into his pocket. Then he steps forward, rubbing his hands together, breathing out a cloud of air. "Now for some leg rubbing."

I laugh as he backs me up against the car then lifts me and sits me down on his lap as he sinks into the driver's seat and shuts the door. He starts rubbing his hands up and down my legs, tickling my thighs and making the air feel sweltering even though it's below zero out. Ethan and Lila start making out in the passenger seat, making these breathless noises, and Micha whispers something about them challenging us and then kisses me roughly.

The next few minutes move by in a blurry haze full of kissing and touching and awkwardness because Lila and Ethan are in the seat next to us doing the same thing. But everyone's too drunk to care and by the time Micha's mom pulls up beside us in Thomas's old pickup, she damn near gets an eyeful.

Thankfully, everyone's clothes are still on when she raps on the window. She makes Micha and I get out, cracking a joke about us acting like teenagers again, almost like she sort of misses it.

Micha and I get in the backseat and Ethan climbs back, too, ungracefully diving over the console. Then Lila follows him, jumping onto his lap. We're crammed in the backseat, Lila's knees pressing against mine as I pretty much ball myself up on Micha's lap.

"There's room up here," Micha's mom says, patting the empty passenger seat and then she adjusts the rearview mirror.

"We're good," the four of us say nearly in sync and then we laugh.

Micha's mom sighs and then follows Thomas out of the parking lot, leaving the bar, Mikey, and our past behind. At least for now.

Chapter Sixteen

Micha

I feel bad about getting wasted, but I was having fun hanging out and drinking beers and shots with Ethan and I got a little carried away. I promise myself that I won't be mean to Ella no matter what and it's actually pretty easy, considering the moment I see her I want to tear off her clothes and bury myself inside her.

As we head back to my house with my mom, our designated driver, like we're a bunch of teenagers again, I can't seem to keep my hands off Ella. I suck on her neck, giving her a hickey as my fingers sneak up her dress. She breathes against my skin as she buries her face against my neck, trying to be quiet. She smells like vodka and vanilla and I bask in the scent, ready to get home because I'm seriously about to lose it.

The only time I get distracted is when we pass by

a group of Christmas carolers standing on the corner near the park, bundled up in hats, coats, and gloves singing at the top of their voices.

"Wait a minute," I say, leaning forward and slapping the console with my hand. "Stop the car."

"Jesus, Micha." My mom flinches in surprise but then starts to tap on the brakes. "What's wrong?"

"We should go throw snowballs at them," I say nodding my head at the carolers and then pinch Ella's leg. "Like we used to do when we were kids every year. It was kind of like our tradition."

"Micha Scott," my mom says in horror. "That's terrible."

But Ella starts to laugh. "I completely forgot about that. Remember that time I hit that guy straight in the face with one and then he chased us for blocks."

"You always got us into so much trouble," I say with a grin. "Let's do it again."

Ella starts to smile and even though we're probably too old to keep carrying on that tradition, we're both drunk enough that we're seriously considering it. But my mom presses on the gas and drives down the road, sighing disappointedly.

"You two and your crazy ideas," she mutters under her breath.

I'm disappointed that she's not letting us, but I quickly forget about it and start kissing Ella again until

195

we're pulling up to my house and my mom is turning off the engine.

"Do you guys want me to make something to eat?" my mom asks as we hop out of the car. "It might be good for you guys to eat something."

"We're good. Thanks again for coming to get us." I wave her off and she sighs as I lead Ella inside, not even bothering to wait for Lila and Ethan or listen when my mom asks me to come back.

By the time I get us to my room and close the door, I'm burning with the need to touch Ella as I flip on the lamp. I don't even give her a warning as I jerk her leather jacket off and throw it onto the floor.

"I'm going to have my hands full tonight, aren't I?" she states with a wicked glint in her eyes like that's exactly what she wants.

I squint at her cheek, grazing my thumb across it. It looks even redder and more swollen in the light. "How hard did that girl hit you?"

She shrugs. "A normal hit." Then she grabs the bottom of my shirt and yanks me toward her. "But it doesn't matter. I got her back twice so everything's good," she says and then smashes her lips into mine so hard I think we'll have bruises in the morning.

I slip my tongue inside her as my fingers wander through her hair, up her body, under her dress, into her panties. I feel her from the inside but only for a moment because it's all that I can take. Then I pull my fingers out of her and peel her tight dress off, chucking it onto the floor, too. She helps me out of my shirt and then undoes the button of my jeans so I can I slip them off. I notice that she only uses her left hand and I wonder if she hurt her other hand when she hit the girl. I'm about to ask her when she unhooks her bra, and all thoughts leave my mind.

I grab her roughly and seal my lips onto hers as I back her up. She gasps against my mouth as her back slams into the wall and my knee bumps against the nightstand, knocking my lap onto the floor. The room goes dark, a small amount of light flowing in from the Christmas lights outside as I stroke her thighs, feeling her skin as I explore every inch of her mouth with my tongue until our lips are swollen and I need air.

As I pull away, she sucks my bottom lip into her mouth hard, tracing her tongue across my lip ring and driving me mad. I groan as she frees my lip and I grind up against her, sucking kisses down her jawline to her neck. I gently bite at her skin, tasting her, rolling my tongue along her flesh as my fingers hook the edge of her panties and she makes these sexy whimpering noises. I move back only to slide them down her legs, and then I yank my boxers off. As I lean into kiss her again, I hear voices from just outside the hall. My mom laughing and Thomas saying something really loud.

Ella and I pause, panting heavily, her chest colliding with mine every time she lets out a breath.

"Maybe we should slow down," she whispers, blinking. "At least until they go to sleep. They might hear us."

"No fucking way," I tell her, seeking a solution where we can be noisy without anyone hearing us. I reach for my iPod and click it on, cranking up the volume of "Change (In the House of Files)," by Deftones, and the music rises over the voices.

"If we can't hear them, I'm sure they can't hear us," I say and then crash my lips into hers again.

Her fingers make a searing path up my back and knot through my hair as I grab her thighs and pick her up, opening her legs and giving her hardly any warning before I sink deep inside her. We gasp as we move our bodies together, holding on to each other like nothing else exists, the sounds of the music drifting in and out of focus until I can't concentrate on anything else but her and how she makes me feel. How just a few years ago, I'd gone out with Ethan to the same pub and come home with a girl who had been hitting on me all night. The sex was meaningless, the passion, heat, sweat, burning raw intensity that I feel with Ella nonexistent.

There was nothing and now there's everything.

After we come down from the high, I gently pull out of her, carrying her weight when her weak legs give out on her. She laughs exhaustedly as I scoop her up in my arms and stumble over to the bed. I lay her down and then climb under the covers with her.

She places her head on my chest and draws heart patterns on my damp skin. "I love you," she whispers.

I shut my eyes and hug her tighter against me. "I love you, too."

We hold on to each other, floating toward sleep, just like we did so many times when we were younger. We actually started sleeping together when we were about thirteen, after we'd been hanging out in my room and Ella didn't want to go home because she was avoiding her family. I let her sleep in my bed with me, not because I was being a pervert but because I liked having her around and didn't want her to go home. My mom worked nightshifts so I knew we wouldn't get caught. It was the best night of sleep I'd had in a long time and after that it started becoming a habit. We alternated nights between our rooms and sometimes at other peoples' houses, on park benches, and some-times even in my car.

The car was actually my favorite place, because it gave me an excuse to lie closer to her. Yes, a lot of amazing things happened in that car. All Ella and I needed was each other and my car and we were good, no matter what life threw at us, even if she was mad at me. We raced in it. We kissed in it. We held each other in it, just like we're holding each other now.

I smile at the memories flooding my head. I start to fall asleep, thinking about the night that started with a fight over a stolen kiss and ended with us falling asleep together, squished in the driver's seat.

It started off as a really shitty night, but in the end it turned out to be one of the best nights of my life.

Chapter Seventeen

Two and a half years ago...

Micha

It's about time to race and I'm nervous, even though I have Ella in the car with me, my little good luck charm. We've been off balance all night, partly because my growing feelings for her are making things awkward since every time I'm around her I keep hoping she'll say she has feelings for me, knowing if I'm the one to tell her first she'll freak out. But not tonight. She's had a rough day and is in a bad mood and even though I want to scream out to her that I'm in love with her, I know I can't. I'm hoping, though, that after the race, we can drive up to our spot and talk for a little while, sitting on the hood of my car, listening to music—it's one of my favorite things to do.

But for now I have to concentrate on racing, so I focus on driving, winning, and making sure Ella has a fun time tonight, despite the fact that I can't stop thinking about kissing her.

"So are you ready for this?" I ask, pumping the gas as she dazes off, staring out the passenger window. She's been doing it most of the night and I wish she would just tell me what's on her mind.

She turns and looks at me. "Ready for what?"

I pump the gas again. "To race. I know how turned on you get over it," I pretend to tease, even though it's true.

She rolls her eyes, for a fleeting second looking happy "Whatever." Then her expression falls and she looks out the window again.

I hesitate. "So do you want to tell me why you've been so quiet all night?"

She shrugs and lets out a loud breath. It grows deafeningly quiet in the car as she breathes in and out. I swallow hard and start to return my attention to the front of me, when suddenly she says, "Micha, can I ask you something?" She sounds choked and nervous and it makes me wonder what the hell she's going to say.

"You know you can ask me anything." I grip the steering wheel, staring ahead at the trees, unable to look at her, praying to fucking God that she'll finally say something, like "Micha, can you feel it, too? Micha, please fuck me now. Micha, I love you."

I'm hoping for the last one, even though it's not really a question, but after a long, drawn-out silence, all she ends up saying is, "What's the bet for the race?" She sighs at the end, like she was going to say something else—maybe something important.

I have to take a deep breath before I speak, otherwise all the emotions on the brink of exploding inside me will show in my voice. "I think, like, a hundred bucks."

"Who are you racing?"

"Danny and his Challenger."

"You're totally going to win it." Her lips turn upward and I think it actually might be a real smile.

I relax as I line up to race. I'm nervous and Ella can tell because she turns up a little "The Distance," by Cake, because she knows it'll settle me down. When the lyrics and beat bump through the speakers, I look at her.

"Only you know the way to my heart," I say with a tense, nervous smile. "Thank you, pretty girl."

"Of course," she replies, relaxing back in the seat, looking comfortable there, like she belongs there, which she does. "What are best friends for?"

I force a smile, then push in the clutch and shove the shifter into first. Danny's in his Challenger to the side of us and he throttles up his engine. I return it, pressing the gas down so hard the car vibrates from the rumble of the engine. Then Danny's girlfriend comes strutting up between the cars. There's a rule that the girlfriend of the instigator of the race has to start the race. When I do it, I always have to pick some random girl from out of the crowd, because I've never had a girlfriend—never wanted one. I've tried to get Ella to do it a few times, but she always rejects me, saying it's a sexist rule, when really I think she's worried people will start to think we're dating, even though a lot of people do already.

"You know you can always tell me to slow down," I tell her, letting her know she's safe. "If you get scared."

"You know I don't get scared." She slips her shoes off and props her feet on the dash for support.

The way she looks so comfortable makes me grin. "I know, but I always want to make sure."

Seconds later, Danny's girlfriend throws down her arms, and just like that we're off, kicking up a large cloud of dust that smothers the audience. The longer we drive, the more relaxed Ella becomes, her head falling back against the headrest and she looks so relaxed as she shuts her eyes and breathes in the cool air blowing through the window. She looks so beautiful at that moment, so touchable, so fucking perfect, and I almost forget I'm racing.

Then I glance at the road and realize the Challenger has died and we're about to slam into it. "Shit," I mutter and one of the gears grinds as I downshift and the tires skid in the dirt, the car swerving a little. I know if I don't get control of the car something bad could easily happen. It's not the first time this sort of thing has happened, but Ella is always the first thing to come to mind, which makes it more important for me to regain control.

"Micha..." Ella says as I crane the wheel to the side and downshift again.

The car fishtails, the back end winding a curvy path against the dirt as we swerve to the right. I hold my breath as we veer sharply around the Challenger and just about over-correct, but I use force to straighten the wheel out. I get it under control, but there's little time for a celebration as the end of the road appears.

"Damn it." I jerk on the e-brake and the tires screech.

We spin out of control, the engine making a lot of noises, but I get everything under control and in the end we're racing back toward the finish line.

I release a breath as I floor the car, even though the Challenger is still stalled.

"Faster or slower?" I ask Ella playfully, because I've pretty much won the race.

She grips the door handle. "Faster of course."

I grin because I'm not surprised by her answer and she laughs as I slam my foot on the gas pedal. The trees and dark sky blur by as the headlights light up the dirt road ahead of us. I shift gears, increasing the speed, and people scatter out of the way, worried I'm going to lose control because sometimes it happens. But I easily make it over the finish line, winning, and Ella looks so happy that it makes all the tension between us dissipate.

I smile this really stupid, goofy smile that makes Ella giggle and then I lean my head back against the seat, relaxing for the first time tonight. "Fuck, I thought I was totally going to slam into the back end of him for a moment," I say with a laugh.

"I didn't," she says and I turn my head and give her a doubtful look, but still smile. "What? I knew you had him."

"*We* had him," I say. "And *we* have one hundred bucks to split." I get really excited over the fact that I just won and she's with me and she's smiling, which was sort of the whole point of the night anyway. "Fuck, fuck, fuck," I say, amped up as I pound on the steering wheel.

She snorts a laugh. "You're such a goofball." She laughs a little more and I swear to God the sound of it is the most amazing thing I've ever heard. Rare and beautiful and it makes me want to touch her so fucking much. Without even thinking, as if it's the most natural thing in the world, I lean over the console and pull her into a hug.

For a second, I worry she's going to flip out on me because she hates getting hugged but she's happy enough at the moment that she hugs me back and I can't help but breathe in the scent of her. It's intoxicating, along with her warmth and, God, I get so swept away in her, wanting to touch her, kiss her, be inside her. Before I even know what I'm doing, I tilt my head to the side and press my lips to hers. I don't even know why I do it—I'm usually more careful—but I slip up and I know it the second our lips touch and she tenses, sucking in a sharp breath.

I panic and before she can say anything, I pull back and get out of the car. I've seriously fucked up, not just because I know she's going to be upset with me, but because I took a happy moment and ruined it.

Shit.

I procrastinate as long as I can, celebrating and collecting my money from Danny and then we chat a little while about cars and other stupid shit, but I barely pay attention, distracted by the lingering sensation of Ella's warm lips on mine. Yeah, I know I messed up but, God, the taste of her was so incredible.

Ella sits in the Chevelle for what seems like forever and then she finally gets out and goes and hangs with Renee and Kelly, even though she doesn't really like Renee. Ella was obviously in a bad mood when I'd woken her up from her nap earlier, but my kissing her only made it worse.

As I'm chatting with Danny, Trixie something-or-other comes up behind me and whispers in my ear that we should go to my car and hang out alone. I briefly consider it, but all I can think about is Ella and I know it's time to go face her wrath. I decline Trixie's offer and walk up to Ethan's truck, where Ella's sitting on the tailgate arguing with him, while Renee and Kelly share a bottle of vodka.

"Knock it off." Ella puts her hands on her hips, giving Ethan the death glare. "You're trying to pick a fight with me."

Ethan shakes his head as he takes a swig of beer. "Bullshit. You're just in a pissy mood as usual."

"Hey, you ready to go?" I interrupt, playfully nudging Ella's foot with mine like nothing happened, like we didn't just kiss.

"If you are," Ella replies, her expression undecipherable, so I have no idea what the hell she's thinking. She jumps off the tailgate and walks past a row of cars, heading to the Chevelle parked over by a tree.

She's wearing a pair of cutoffs and it's hard not to stare at her ass the entire time. I know if she looks back and catches me checking her out things will only get worse, but I take the risk and only look away from her when she gets into the car.

"Good luck with that." Ethan rolls his eyes as Renee hands him the bottle of vodka. "What the hell did you do to her? She's even bitchier than she normally is."

I release an uneasy breath. "I fucked up," I say and then turn for the car, feeling bad about kissing her, but the way she tasted was so fucking mind-blowing, it makes it hard to regret.

I prepare myself before I pull open the car door and climb inside with her. I slam the door and the soundlessness that follows is unnerving.

"Do you want me to drive slow or fast back home?" I try to make light as I put the keys in the ignition and turn over the engine.

She slowly turns her head toward me. "I thought we were going to our spot?" she asks, surprising me. I'd honestly thought that idea had gone out the window for tonight because I thought she'd be too pissed off.

I shove the shifter into drive and tap on the gas while pushing down on the brake, revving the engine. "You still want to go?"

She shrugs as I turn the headlights on, lighting up

the trees in front of us. "If you still want to go." Her eyes are unreadable in the dark, but I can tell by the silent plea in her tone that she doesn't want to go home.

"Of course I do," I tell her, then I release the brake and peel out onto the road. "I was just making sure you still do."

"You said I had to," she reminds me. "That you weren't going to let me sulk around at my house all night."

"I know…but I'm giving you an out." *As a sorry-for-kissing-you-even-though-I'm-not-really-sorry.*

"I don't want an out." She stares out the window with her arms crossed over her chest. She has the same tank top on as the one she was wearing when I woke her up, only she put a bra on, so sadly I can't see the outline of her nipples anymore. But I do notice how forcefully her chest is moving up and down. She's anxious and I don't think it's just because of the kiss. In fact, whatever is making her anxious now is probably the thing that had her sleeping in her bed at three o'clock in the afternoon.

I don't say anything else and drive in the direction of our spot, a secluded area in the middle of the trees beside the lake. By the time we get there it's past midnight and Ella's drifting off to sleep. I park the car not too far away from the water, and then silence the engine but leave the headlights on.

Ella blinks and sits up, quiet for a while as she stares out at the water. Finally she reaches her arm across the console and turns the key back over, so the battery turns on. Then she picks up the iPod from the dashboard and turns on some Spill Canvas, before getting out of the car. She treads up to the shore, stopping just before she arrives at the water, then crosses her arms and looks up at the stars, her hair blowing in the light summer breeze.

I climb out of the car and cautiously walk up to the side of her. The moonlight reflects in her eyes as she bites on her bottom lip, refusing to look at me. I consider saying sorry for kissing her, but it'd be a lie and I fucking hate lying to her.

"My mom had one of her episodes today," she says quietly, breaking the silence as she hugs herself. "She was looking for a picture of when we all went to the beach, even though we never have. I spent all day looking for it, even though I knew I'd never find it and finally I had to just lie to her and tell her I think I lost the photo, so she'd let it go." She closes her eyes and breathes in deep. "And I was so glad when she finally fell asleep...so fucking relieved. I'm the worst daughter in the world."

"No, you're not." I sweep her hair off her shoulder and she stiffens when my fingers brush against the back of her neck. "You're a hell of a lot better than most daughters."

She shakes her head as she swallows hard. "No, I'm not. I get so tired of it...all of it. Sometimes I just want it to all stop." She pauses, catching her breath.

I rack my brain for something to say to her that'll make her feel better, but I'm not sure it's words I'm looking for. So I back away from her and she doesn't look at me, her eyes fixed ahead. When I reach the car, I open the door and lean inside to get the iPod. Then I shuffle through the songs until I stumble onto one of the slower, softer classics and then I crank up the volume and hike down toward her again.

She looks over her shoulder at me as the music floods the forest around us. I stick out my hand, letting her know what I want to do, because we've done it before and I'm sure we'll do it again. She stares at my hand undecidedly before she guardedly moves over to me, her expression impartial.

"You're such an old man with your music sometimes," she says, stopping just out of my reach, her arms still folded over her chest.

I keep my hand extended to her and force a grin, even though I'm a little nervous. "Hey, 'Girl from the North Country' is a classic. And it's got Johnny Cash and Bob Dylan."

"It's old-man music." Her tone is tinged with humor. "Because inside, you're an old man."

"Then that would make you an old lady for hanging out with me."

She rolls her tongue, restraining a smile. I grab hold of her hand and jerk on her arm, tugging her against me and her laughter slips through. The sound breaks the tension between us and I know I'm off the hook for now.

I twirl her around a few times and she laughs even harder, her hair falling in her face as she stumbles to keep up with me. I continue to twirl her until I know she's dizzy, like when we were kids and we'd hang out in my backyard, spinning in circles.

"Micha, please stop," she begs, laughing and stumbling over her feet. "I can't see straight."

I stop and she crashes against me. She clutches on to my shoulders, holding on to me for support as I slip my arms around her and rock us to the rhythm, supporting her weight. My palm makes a path down her back, stopping when I near her ass, knowing I can't push things any further, at least not tonight.

She relaxes her head against my chest and I breathe in the vanilla scent of her hair. "You're too nice to me sometimes," she says. "In fact, you spoil me. You should really stop."

I leave one hand on her back and move the other to her head and hold her against me. "You deserve to be spoiled," I say, because no one else will except for me. No one's ever made her feel special, given her birthday presents, taken her places, and I'm pretty sure neither her mother nor her father have told her they love her. That became my job the moment I got her to climb over the fence.

"Feeling better?" I ask her, kissing the top of her head.

"I am," she says, her hands sliding up my shoulders and hitching around the back of my neck. "But Micha?"

I try to remain calm, but it's difficult when she's touching me like this. "Yeah."

"If you ever kiss me on the lips again without permission," she says, "I'll kick you in the balls."

I snort a laugh. "Okay, sounds fair."

She pinches the back of my neck and another laugh escapes me. "I'm being serious."

"I know you are." And I'm sure she's telling the truth but I'm just relieved she's letting it go.

She doesn't say anything else and I hold on to her until the song finishes. The next song turns on and we keep dancing, not stopping until five more songs have played through. I pull back only when I feel her weight lean heavy against me, like she's falling asleep. When I look down at her, her eyes are shut and her grip on me is loosening.

"We should probably get you home," I say, brushing her hair back from her forehead.

She shakes her head with her eyes shut. "I don't want to go home."

"Then where do you want to go?" I ask. "Back to my house?"

She yawns. "Can't we just stay here?"

I stand there while she starts to drift off to sleep in my arms. Finally, I lean her back, slip my arms underneath her legs, and pick her up. She's too tired to argue with me and instead nestles against me as I carry her back to the car. Then I maneuver the door open and lower us both into the driver's seat.

"Do you want to get in the backseat?" I ask, sitting her up so I can get my legs in and then shut the door.

She shakes her head. "I just want to sleep right here."

There's limited space, but in the end it doesn't matter how much room there is because she's in my arms and she wants to be there. So holding onto her, I recline the chair back and lie down. She shifts her weight, so she's to the side of me, our legs entangled as she rests her head on my chest. As the music continues to play, we drift off to sleep together.

Chapter Eighteen

Present day...

Ella

When I open my eyes to daylight, Micha's already awake, with my mom's journal on his lap with the photo of her beside his leg. He's leaning against the headboard with his boxers on and he's shirtless so I can see his lean muscles and wisps of his hair dangling across his forehead. There's an intense look on his face as he reads the pages but when I move to sit up, my head and cheek pulsating in protest, he closes the journal, the intensity shifting to ease.

"Anything good in there?" I ask, clutching the blanket over my bare chest.

He shrugs, but by his frown I can tell he hasn't found anything that's happy. He tucks the photo into the journal, marking the page before he puts it aside, and then reaches over to stroke my puffy, tender cheekbone. "We should have put some ice on that last night," he says. "Seriously, Ella, it looks like it hurts like hell."

I place my hand over his. "It does hurt like hell."

"Do you want to tell me how it really happened?" he asks, and when I tense he adds, "I know when you're lying, Ella May, so don't try to tell me some girl hit you because I could tell last night that you were full of shit."

"Then why didn't you call me out on it?"

"Because I was thinking with my dick and nothing else."

I smile, thinking about how he pushed me up against the wall and slammed into me so hard I could feel it through my entire body. "My legs actually hurt a little from last night," I divulge as I move the blankets off me and massage my thighs.

He looks down at my legs with intensity in his eyes. "I could say I feel bad, but I don't."

I cover myself back up with the blanket and lie down on the bed. He lies down with me and props his elbow on the pillow and rests his head against his hand.

"I'll tell you," I say as his finger strokes my cheek, "but you have to promise me that you won't do anything about it. No going looking for a fight."

217

He stops moving his fingers. "I won't promise that."

"Then I won't tell you."

"Ella May—"

I cover his mouth with my hand and cut him off. "Don't 'Ella May' me. The last thing I need is a husband who either gets charges pressed against him or ends up seriously injured."

He pauses and then his lips curve upward beneath my hand. "Say it again."

"Only if you promise."

"Fine." He sighs and my hand leaves his mouth. "I won't go looking for a fight as long as you'll tell me what happened and call me your husband again." He gets this goofy grin on his face that makes me smile.

"All right, husband," I say, making his smile expand. I take a deep breath and tell him about Mikey. I can see for the entire time that he's working really hard to control his reaction, his hands balling into fists as he listens.

When I'm finished, he's quiet for a while, and then he finally says, "Can I at least have Ethan kick his ass?"

I shake my head. "No. Lila doesn't need him hurt either. Or in jail."

His jaw is set tight and his eyes linger on my cheek before he blows out a breath. "I really want to beat the shit out of him, Ella May. I swear to God..." He clenches his fists, the muscles in his lean arms tightening.

"I know you do," I say. "But I don't want you to."

"You're killing me," he says, aggravated.

"I know, but it's for the best," I explain. "Besides, I got a good kick and hit in."

"He should have never hit a girl...I swear to God..." He blows out a frustrated breath, shaking his head. "Can't I at least fuck up his car or something?"

"He'll probably think it was you," I say. "Or me."

"Please, you have to give me something."

I sigh. "Fine, we can sneak over to his house and slash his tires one night before we go home."

"That's it?" He pouts, frowning. "Can't I, like, smash in his windows and then hit him a few times?"

"Just the tires," I say. "And no hitting. I don't want this turning into a huge problem."

His frown deepens. "Fine, but only for you."

"Thank you." I give him a kiss and he still seems irritated, but he responds, sliding his tongue into my mouth. We keep kissing as he flips us over, rolling me onto my back and lying over me. He gazes down at me all lovey-dovey, stroking my cheek with a thoughtful look on his face, and when he opens his mouth, I have no idea what he's going to say.

"Lila says you got me a Christmas present," he says, surprising me.

I shake my head. "Only because she made me get you one, so don't think you have to get me anything. I know we don't do the whole Christmas thing."

"What if I want to get you something, though?"

"Then you can," I say. "But just so you know, what I got you isn't anything great." Which is true. While we were out shopping for wedding decorations, I saw these friendship bracelets that looked exactly like the ones Micha and I had for a while when we were kids, after we made this promise to be best friends forever. Eventually they got all worn out and we threw them away or lost them, and when I told Lila this, she said I should get them and give them to Micha as a present. I'm not one for sappiness, but I still found myself buying them.

"I'm already getting you," he says. "Which is the best present ever."

I shake my head, and can't help but smile. "You're so cheesy sometimes."

"And you secretly love it."

I don't respond because he's right and then he grins as he nudges my legs open with his knee, shifting his hips between them, ready to slip back inside me.

But a knock on the door interrupts us.

"Ella," Lila calls out from the other side.

"Just ignore her," Micha whispers, nibbling on my earlobe as he grazes his thumb across my nipple.

I groan, squeezing my legs against his hips as the tip of him presses into me.

"Ella, I know you're in there and I need you to come out." She pauses. "Dean and Caroline are here."

I work to keep my voice level as Micha thrusts inside me. "I'll be out in just a second." My voice comes out breathless and Micha laughs, his mouth hovering over mine.

He pauses, arching his brow. "A second. Really?"

I reach around and pinch his ass, causing him to laugh. "You better make it a second, otherwise you're going to get blue balls for the rest of the day."

Shaking his head, he smiles. "Fine, you win." Then his slips all the way inside me and again I lose myself in him.

∽

About fifteen minutes later, we're fully dressed and we head out to the kitchen, exhausted but content. Lila's at the kitchen table, dressed in her pajamas with little cherries on the fabric. The table and counters are still covered in ribbon and candles, along with a few boxes of cereal and dirty dishes. Ethan's in the chair beside her, in a T-shirt and plaid pajama bottoms, eating a bowl of cereal.

A knowing grin rises on Lila's face when she sees us. "Took you two long enough," she jokes as she adds a spoonful of sugar to her coffee.

Ethan glances over his shoulder, his eyes bloodshot, probably because he's hungover. He stares at my cheek, which I tried to cover up with makeup, but shiners on the face are pretty much a lost cause so all I can do is wear it proudly.

"Who the hell beat you up?" Ethan asks, stirring his cereal with a spoon.

I touch the spot with my fingers as Micha releases my hand and goes over to the coffeepot beside the sink. "Mikey," I tell him.

Ethan lets out a gradual exhale. "Shit, was it because..."

He trails off as Micha hands me a cup of coffee. "Because you two jackasses threw a shake in his car?" he says. "Yep."

Ethan frowns as he rakes his fingers through his hair, making it stick up on the top. "Hey, it wasn't my idea."

"Yeah, it was mine," I say to Micha, inhaling the aroma of the coffee. "Don't give him credit for my awesomeness."

"I'm too hungover for you two to start arguing." Micha grimaces as he stretches his arms above his head, the bottom of his shirt riding up, flaunting his muscles.

Ethan and I exchange a challenging look, and then Ethan gives up and returns to eating his cereal as I take a soothing gulp of my coffee.

"You said Caroline and Dean were here?" I ask Lila as I sit down at the table.

Lila nods as she stirs her coffee. Her hair is pulled back in a short ponytail and she doesn't have any makeup on. "They were, but I told them you were going to be a minute so they went over to your house and I told them I'd send you over when you came out."

Out the window, I see there's a large maroon SUV parked in the driveway beside my house, just behind the Firebird. "Is that their rental car?" I ask.

Lila shakes her head. "No, they drove here because Caroline didn't want to fly. I think it's their car."

"I guess he got rid of the Porsche then," I say, adding a drop of milk to my coffee.

"Probably because they're about to have a baby and there's no room for a car seat in a Porsche." Lila smiles and then takes a gulp from her coffee mug. "Caroline's belly is so cute."

Ethan shakes his head, his eyes wide as he fixes

them on his cereal. I glance over at Micha, who's watching me while he leans against the counter, sipping his coffee. When he pulls the mug away from his mouth, he licks his lips. I know him well enough to know that he's attempting to read my reaction, not just about the Porsche—my mom's old car—being sold, but because Lila's talking about babies.

I rise to my feet and look at Micha. "Do you want to come with me and say hi or something?"

Micha nods and moves away from the counter for the back door. We grab our coats and tell Lila and Ethan we'll be right back, and then we head over to my house. Thomas's old truck is parked in the driveway behind Micha's Chevelle and there are shoe prints in the snow, leading from Micha's steps to the fence. Then they pick up on the other side of the fence, heading to the stairs of my house. I can't help but smile because it probably means Dean and Caroline took our little path to the house.

I point down at the tracks. "Hey look, all the cool kids are doing it now," I joke.

Micha grabs the top of the fence and hops gracefully over it, landing in the snowbank on the other side. "I'd rather they not. I like that it's our path and I want it to stay that way."

"Me too," I agree, sliding my fingers around the

'icy metal fence and hoisting myself up. Halfway over, Micha grabs onto my hips and helps me to the ground, setting me in the driveway so I don't sink in the snowbank.

We tromp through the snow to the house and walk inside, the air smelling like cinnamon and perfume, along with a hint of bacon. There are pans on the stove and there's coffee brewing in a pot on the counter.

I should have prepared myself more because as soon as we enter, Caroline practically starts jumping up and down. She's wearing a flowing purple dress and her black hair is braided. The fabric of the dress stretches over her protruding belly and even though I try not to, I can't help but stare. Dean is sitting on the table, his feet propped up on a chair with a newspaper on his lap. He's dressed in a collared shirt and slacks and I still can't get used to the look. Growing up, all he would wear were old T-shirts and jeans and he even dyed his hair blue once.

"Oh my God, there you two are," Caroline says excitedly, clapping her hands with enough energy to power the entire house. "Congrats, you two."

"Thanks." I force myself not to get awkward and I let the nice moment be, even though deep down I feel uncomfortable with the positive attention.

She pauses. "Ella, what happened to your face?"

I cup my swollen cheek. "I got into a small fight, but nothing major."

"Just like old times," Dean remarks with a shake of his head.

"Well, I hope you're okay," Caroline says, examining my cheek.

"I'm fine," I assure her. "The swelling will go down in a day or two."

"Good, then it'll be gone for the wedding." She leans in to hug me and I uncomfortably hug her back, feeling her belly press against mine. When she moves away, she notices me staring and places her hand across her stomach.

"It's a girl," she says and Dean glances up at me with a strange look on his face that I can't decipher. I wonder if he's freaked out, too, at the thought of children, if he's worried he'll end up like our father, drunk and nonexistent. I could ask him, but we're not to that place yet.

"Congratulations," I say to both of them.

"Thanks." Dean folds up the newspaper and tosses it into the table by the cookie jar. He's quiet for a moment and I seriously have no idea what the hell's going to come out of his mouth. "You, too."

I'm surprised by his simple remark and I miss a beat before I respond. "Thanks."

"This is going to be so good," Caroline says, hurrying over to the counter to a plate of eggs and bacon. "A wedding outside at Christmas time near a lake. I can only imagine the pictures I'm going to get to take." She starts munching on the bacon.

"It'll be freezing though," Dean says, stating the obvious as he hops off the table and then strides up to Caroline and circles an arm around her waist. "You sure you don't want to have it inside? We'll all be freezing our asses off by the end of it."

Micha and I exchange a look and then we both shake our heads. "No, cold temperature or not, I'm not having it anywhere else," I tell Dean, and Micha squeezes my hand. "It's important."

"Okay," Dean says, confused. "I guess we're having an outdoor wedding. But who all's coming?"

"Me, Micha, Lila, Ethan," I ramble off the list, counting down on my fingers. "Micha's mom and boyfriend, you and Caroline obviously, and Dad…and maybe his girlfriend."

"Oh yeah," Dean says as he kisses Caroline's shoulder. "The secretary."

"So you knew about her?"

His shoulders rise and fall as he shrugs. "He mentioned it on the phone a couple of weeks ago."

He never mentioned it to me. "Oh."

Sensing my downward mood, Micha takes my hand and gives me a soothing kiss on the cheek, his unshaven jawline rough against my skin, but comforting at the same time. Dean doesn't seem to notice at all that something's bothering me, and it's not his fault. He doesn't know me like Micha does—no one in my family does.

"That's not very many people," Caroline says, picking up a fork from off the plate. "Are you sure you don't want to have more? I mean, you've got to have some more old friends still around who'd like to come to it. I know it's short notice but people might still come if you invited them."

I shake my head. "I don't have anyone else I want to invite."

She frowns down at her eggs as she stabs them with the fork. "What about you, Micha?"

"I'm good with just Ella there," Micha answers, hugging me against his chest. "No offense, but I really don't care if anyone else is there."

Caroline sighs as she takes a bite of the eggs. "Well, I guess we'll start planning then."

"Lila and Micha's mom have already done a lot," I tell her. "I don't think there's that much left to do."

Caroline smiles at me as Dean lets her go and heads to the fridge. "Oh, Ella, there's always more to do," Caroline assures me. "Trust me."

And she's right, but only because I'm not planning the wedding myself. If it were just me, I'd have Micha, me, the minister, and no one else. The wedding would take place somewhere serenely beautiful like at a private beach or in a field of violets. I would wear something punk/gothic and Micha would wear black with his leather bands because he always looks so God damn sexy when he wears all black. And there would be no vows, just exchanges of "I do" and a kiss.

But I'm not planning the wedding myself. I have a whole team of people who are eager to make everything beautiful and sparkly.

I end up spending the rest of the day with Lila, Caroline, and Micha's mom in the next town over so that Micha's mom can pick out a dress. Caroline buys one too and then purchases a necklace for me to wear even though I tell her I don't need one. She tried to buy me a veil at first but there was no way in hell I was going to walk around with a piece of cloth on my head attached to a diamond tiara. So she ends up buying these clips that have black roses in them to match the dress and then we go to a cake shop and order a cake. The whole thing is getting a little too fancy for me, but I let them go crazy because it's making them happy and it's not really hurting anything. Thankfully, Caroline has the same sort of gothic style as me and orders a black- and red-striped cake with this lace on the bottom and red roses on the top. It matches the red and black ribbons and candles we already have for decorations, which Lila insists we can string up on the tree branches, although I'm a little doubtful they'll stay up, especially if it's snowing.

At the end of the day, I'm exhausted, but in a good, strange sort of way, like I may have accomplished something important, like finally committing to the wedding by being part of the planning. Plus, I'd always wondered what it would be like to have people in my life, even though I actually wouldn't admit it aloud. A few years ago, if I was capable of looking forward and seeing myself getting married, I'd imagine myself taking everything on alone and being miserable the entire time, feeling lonely and empty.

But right now I feel whole, yet still sad because there's one person missing from the scene. Someone who can't be here and it makes my heart hurt because if it weren't for my mistake she might have been. I know my mom's death wasn't my fault but it took a lot of therapy to get there and despite the fact that I'm not holding onto my guilt anymore, I still know deep down in my heart that perhaps if I would have stayed home that night, my mom wouldn't have taken her own life and maybe, just maybe, she would have also been out shopping for wedding stuff with me.

When I get back to Micha's house, Micha, Ethan, and my brother are still gone, looking for tuxes to rent at the last minute, even though I suggested they all just wear black button-down shirts. As Lila, Caroline, and Micha's mom get situated in the kitchen, ready to tie more ribbon and put candles in the glass jars they bought, I decide that I need to go visit the cemetery. So I grab my sketchpad and a pencil and bundle up in my coat, gloves, and boots.

When I return to the kitchen, Micha's mom turns around from the sink and notices my outdoor attire. "Ella, where are you headed?" she asks, scrubbing down a plate with a sponge as she holds it under running water.

I tuck my sketchpad under my arm. "I need to go somewhere."

She looks out the window at the cloudy sky and then at the microwave where the time blinks 4:02. "But it's getting dark and colder."

"I won't be gone for too long," I assure her, walking toward the back door.

Lila gives me a strange look from the kitchen table as she loops some ribbon into a bow. "Do you want company?"

They look at me as I open the back door and let the winter air inside. "No. There's something I have to do." I wave at them. "I'll be back soon. I promise." Before either of them can argue, I step outside and shut the door. Heading down the driveway, I pull the top of my jacket over my mouth and nose as the frosty air bites at my skin.

At the end of the driveway, I veer to the right and walk down the sidewalk toward the cemetery, keeping a steady pace, knowing that I'm not going to be able to endure the icy air for very long. By the time I reach the cemetery, my fingers are numb, but I shake off the cold as I sit down in the snow in front of her headstone. There's a leafless tree just behind it and icicles dangle from the bare branches. The iron gate that borders the cemetery is frosted with snow that also covers the tops of some of the headstones.

I relax back on my hands as the snow seeps through my jeans and stare at her gray headstone, trying to gather my thoughts. "I'm not even sure what to say," I say aloud, my breath fogging out in front of me. "I know I should come visit more, but I don't live here any longer." I set my sketchpad and pencil aside and lean forward, resting my arms on my knees. "So I moved to California...I have a home and everything, which is weird, but nice, I guess." I breathe in and breathe out. "Everything is nice really." I pause. "I'm sorry you never got your nice...I started reading your journal and I was hoping it'd have something nice in it, but there isn't anything, not really." I shut my eyes as the cold air kisses my cheek. "I really would like to know if you ever did get any sort of happy. I know Dad said he thinks that you might have been happy sometimes, but he didn't sound like he fully believed it. And I know that you can fake it because that's what I do sometimes. I actually used to do it a lot, but not so much anymore...anymore when I'm happy. I think it's real." My words are true, real, honest. I want to know if she was ever really happy, but maybe it's better not knowing since maybe the answer's not what I want to hear. Maybe she'd tell me no, that she was never happy—not ever. Not when she was younger, when she got married, had kids. I've been in that place where depression was everything but it's not my life anymore and I couldn't even begin to imagine not getting a glimpse of happiness that I feel now. If depression was *all* she ever had then it would be sad and tragic and heartbreaking.

"Completely off the subject, but I'm supposed to be writing vows," I say to my mom's headstone, wishing she could really hear me. "But writing's never been my thing." I press my pencil to the paper and then I draw a line down it, letting my hands move freely. "Drawing was more of my thing." Another line and then another. "I'm not sure if you knew that. I know you raised me and everything, but we never really talked, at least about life and stuff. I never even knew you liked to draw until I got a box from your mom with some of your drawings in it. Well, she didn't exactly send it to me—her lawyer did. She actually passed away. I'm not sure how I feel about that, either. I mean, I didn't know her, yet at the same time it's sort of sad she's gone." I make a few shadings and some curves and jagged lines. When I pull the pencil away, I've drawn Micha's face, half shaded, then below it I write, *My light in my dark life.* I turn the page and draw another quick image. It's nothing fancy but that's okay because fancy's not the point right now. When I'm finished, I have a picture of him holding his guitar, music notes surrounding him. Below it I write, *His mouth warmed my soul.* I draw another one and write, *God, I feel so loved sometimes I forget how to breathe.* Then I start moving the pencil over the paper again, creating a map of our life, the first time we slept together in the same bed, the fence, his car, the concerts, the New Orleans trips, the lake, even the bridge. Not all the lines are perfect, but it's the little flaws and imperfections that make the story so beautiful. I finish off the last drawing, which is solely of Micha and write, *My everything.* Then I close the sketchpad and get to my feet, dusting the snow off the back of my jeans, my ass frozen and numb.

I know that if I'm going to turn it in for my final portfolio, I'm going to have to do more work on it, but the start is there, the basis, and I can build on it from there. Besides, starting is always the hardest part and even though I know everything won't just easily fall into place, at least I know that it's headed toward a completion.

A potentially wonderful completion.

Chapter Nineteen

Micha

When I return home from tux shopping, without a tux, because apparently there's nowhere around Star Grove that has them, Ella's not at the house. My mom tells me she went out on foot somewhere with her sketchbook, which worries me.

"Do you know where she went?" I ask her, sitting down on the sofa beside her as she works on wrapping a Christmas present.

She shakes her head. "No, but it couldn't have been too far, right? Since she walked."

Maybe, but maybe not.

My mom secures a piece of tape on the Christmas present and then sticks a bow on it. "There, I think I've finally got everything wrapped." She leans back to put the Christmas present below the small artificial tree in the corner.

I frown as I slump back in the sofa. "Why is everyone so into presents all of a sudden? We never made a big deal about them before. First Ella and now you."

"So...what's wrong with changing things and giving presents?"

"Because I didn't get anyone anything."

"Are you really worried about everyone or just Ella?"

I sigh. "She got me something and it feels like I should give her something back, but I don't want it to be something stupid—I want it to mean something."

My mom eyes me over for a moment and then she gets to her feet. "Get your coat on and follow me."

"Why?"

"Just do it." She uses her stern voice and I get to my feet.

We put on our coats and then she heads outside, taking Ella's and my path and climbing over the fence to get to Ella's yard. I follow her, totally confused because she's acting weird. Then we wind around the Firebird and step up the back stairs to the door and she knocks, which makes things even weirder because I've rarely knocked before. I usually just walk in.

"Mom, seriously, what are we doing?" I ask, stuffing my hands into my pockets.

My mom knocks again and then turns to me,

shivering from the cold. "A few weeks ago, I saw Raymond carrying out a bunch of boxes to the garage. I offered him some help and we got to talking and he told me that the boxes had some of Ella's mom's old stuff."

"Okay? I'm not following you, Mom."

She smiles at me. "I'm thinking that Ella would probably really like something that belonged to her mom, maybe something she could wear at the wedding."

I open my mouth to tell her this is by far the worst idea she's ever had, since Ella's dad gets weird talking about stuff like that and I'm not even sure how Ella would react if I gave her something of her mom's since it's such an emotional subject for her. But before I can say anything, the door opens up.

"Hey, Terri," Mr. Daniels says, looking confused as to why the two of us would be standing on his doorstep.

"Hey, Raymond," my mom says with a smile. "I have a huge favor to ask you."

I shake my head. My mom hasn't always been this way—so pushy. Well, she sort of has, considering it was her idea for Ella and me to get married in the first place, but she seems to be getting pushier the older she gets.

Raymond's brows crease and my mom starts explaining the little Christmas present dilemma. I feel my insides wind into knots, worried that it's going to upset him and he's going to take it out on Ella. I know they've been good and everything, but still I can't shake the past and the things I've seen.

And when my mom says, "So we were wondering if maybe there was something of Maralynn's we could give her, maybe in one of those boxes I helped you put in the garage a few weeks ago?"

He scratches his head, looking really uncomfortable. "I'm not really sure there is. I mean, most of that stuff was just old clothes of hers."

I tug on my mom's sleeve and say to Mr. Daniels, "No worries, we'll figure something else out."

My mom ignores me, keeping her feet planted. "There's not even, like, a piece of her jewelry or something? Like some earrings that were hers?"

Raymond looks even more uneasy and I'm about to walk off and leave her there when suddenly he stands up straighter and looks over at the garage.

"Hold on...I think I just thought of something." He leans back into the house and grabs a large coat, slipping it on along with a beanie before he steps out and shuts the door. We follow him to the garage and my mom shoots me a grin, like, Ha-ha, I was right, and I shake my head but smile.

When we get inside the garage, Mr. Daniels flips on

the lights and heads over to a stack of boxes in the corner. He lifts up the top box and sets it aside and then stares at the box below it for a moment, almost as if he's afraid to open it. I glance at my mom, who swallows hard, looking a bit uneasy. But then Mr. Daniels relaxes a little and carefully opens the box. He rummages around inside it for a moment and then he takes out this small wooden box. When he turns around, he's holding it in his hand like it's something really important.

"We didn't have a real wedding, you know," he says, looking up from the box. "We barely even dressed up."

My mom nods understandingly. "Micha's father and I got married at a park and I think there was, like, a total of ten guests."

"We only had two," Mr. Daniels says. "They were both my friends, and the only reason we invited them was so they'd be our witnesses. Maralynn didn't want to have anyone else there." He takes a deep breath and sighs. "But anyway," he says, and extends his arm toward me, urging me to take the wooden box. "I gave this to Ella's mom the morning of our wedding. It's not anything fancy. I actually bought it at a pawnshop for, like, twenty-five bucks, but she wore it when we got married and maybe you can give it to Ella and have her do the same."

The box creaks as I open it. Inside there's a black ribbon threaded through a small red rose pendant.

"It's a necklace," Mr. Daniels tells me. "Ella's mom had a thing for roses. I'm not sure if Ella will even want to wear it, but it doesn't hurt to try."

Discounting the fact that Ella might get a little emotional about it being her mom's, if this were a normal necklace, I could see her wearing it with pride.

"Thanks," I say, shutting the box. "I'm sure she'll like it and I'm sure she'll be glad that you gave it to her."

Mr. Daniels nods, and then without saying any more we leave the garage. He and my mom chat at the back door for a little while about nothing major as I stare at the sky noting that it's turning gray and wondering if Ella came home while we were in the garage. I decide to go check and say thanks again to Mr. Daniels before I head back over to my house. When I walk in, Lila and Ethan tell me that she's not there and that they're getting ready to go visit his parents for a while, even though he doesn't want to. They head out and I go into my room and hide the necklace. Then, trying to distract myself, I read some of her mom's journal. Page after page of dark thoughts:

I can't do this. Be a mother and a wife. I thought I could but now I feel like I need to run, flee, escape the fear of commitment on foot. Because it's either escape or wait until Raymond decides he's had enough of me and abandons me. It's inevitable. I can feel it. He'll leave me because really I'm not good enough and sometimes I don't want to be good enough. It's too much work and takes too much strength and I'm so tired.

Maybe I should just run away and leave it all behind.

I really should.

Her words pierce at my chest because if I didn't know any better, I'd swear Ella had written them. But I don't believe that Ella will run away again. She loves me and I know that, even if she has a hard time expressing her feelings. I know she wants to be with me. *She* moved the ring to her engagement finger and moved in with me. She won't run.

She can't.

I keep reading through and my mom sticks her head into my room to tell me she's heading out with Thomas to get some dinner.

"Do you want anything?" she asks me.

I shake my head. "No, thanks."

"Well, there are some leftovers in the fridge if you get hungry," she says.

"Thanks," I say and she smiles and then starts to shut the door.

"And Mom?"

She pauses. "Yeah."

"Thanks for going over to the Danielses and doing that," I say.

She smiles. "No problem. I'm just glad we found you something good to give her."

"Me too," I tell her.

When she leaves, I glance at the clock and decide to give Ella fifteen more minutes before I go searching for her. I continue reading the journal, periodically checking the clock. The next several pages are equally depressing and my heart starts to feel heavy in my chest. It's like I'm reading about a downward spiral, but fortunately I'm the one reading it, not Ella. It was her choice not to, which makes her so much stronger than all this darkness, because she knew it would probably bring her down and she chose not to let it—she chose to be happy.

I'm about to put the journal away when I realize there's only one more page left and I decide to read it so I can be done with it. But then I'll have to go and break the news to Ella that I couldn't find anything happy inside the journal. Hopefully it won't crush her heart.

But as I read over the last page the heaviness dissipates and the words kind of make me smile. After I finish reading it, I get up to go look for Ella because I'm worried about her being gone for so long and because she needs to read this. I put my jacket on and head to the back door where I left my boots, but as I'm crossing the kitchen, the door opens and a breeze gusts inside. Ella enters looking as frozen as a Popsicle, her lips blue, her cheeks kissed pink, and she's shivering.

She offers me a small smile as she shuts the back door behind her. "Were you going somewhere?" she asks, eyeing my coat as she hugs her sketchbook to her chest.

"Yeah, to look for you." I stop zipping up my jacket and place my hands on her cheeks, which are ice-cold. "God, you're freezing. How long were you out there?"

She looks over at the clock on the microwave. "A couple of hours."

"Jesus, Ella." I take the sketchbook and set it aside on the counter. Then I tug off her gloves, gather her hands in mine, and breathe on them while I try to rub warmth back into her.

She smiles up at me. "How was your day of tux shopping?"

"As good as any other day of shopping. Although we didn't get tuxes."

"Good," she says. "I've never been a fan of them.

You'll look much better in your jeans and a button-down shirt."

"As long as you think so then I'm okay with it," I tell her, then pause, choosing my next words carefully as my fingers wrap around her wrist. "When I came home I read some more of your mother's journal."

"Oh yeah?" She pretends to be only slightly interested but I feel her pulse accelerate in her wrist. "Find anything good?"

"I did. Do you want to read it?"

Her throat bobs up and down as she swallows hard, and then she looks at the sketchbook on the counter. "Can I wait just a little bit longer? I'm in good mood and I want to stay in one."

"But what I found is good," I promise her. "Trust me."

"I know, but it'll still be hard to read, whether it's good or bad. It still has to do with her and she's gone and it always makes me sad."

How can I argue with that? "If that's what you want, but I promise it's not bad and I really think you need to read it before we get married." I massage her right hand and she winces. "Does your hand hurt?"

She nods, wincing again. "It's the one I punched Mikey in the face with. My knuckles collided with his jaw."

Thinking about Mikey hitting her still gets under my skin, but I force myself to shove it aside because I promised her I wouldn't do anything about it and I refuse to break my promises to her no matter what. "How many times have I told you to hit here?" I free her hand and pound my fist flat against my palm. "Don't use your knuckles."

"I know, but I was drunk and he's a scary guy. I got a little nervous and screwed up the punch," she says and the anger inside me flickers. I was never one for fighting. Sure, I've gotten into a couple of fights but the only major one was with Grantford Davis, who deserved to get his ass kicked.

"What do you want to do for the rest of the night?" I tuck a strand of her auburn hair behind her ear.

She looks around at the empty kitchen. "Where is everyone?"

"Caroline went to your house with Dean. My mom went to dinner and Thomas went out with his friend." I place my hands on her hips. "And Lila and Ethan went out to get something to eat."

"So we have the entire house to ourselves?" she asks with a naughty grin on her face.

I tap my finger on my lip. "Whatever shall we do?"

"Hmmm..." Her eyes sparkle as she collects the sketchpad off the counter. "I have no idea."

I return my hand to her waist and glide my palm around to her ass, cupping it roughly. Her body arches toward me. "Oh, I have a few ideas, starting with you getting naked."

She laughs and then suddenly takes off running toward the hallway, chucking her sketchpad onto the couch as she passes it. "I'll tell you what, I'll get naked when you can find me." She smiles at me, then spins around and disappears down the hallway.

"Oh, pretty girl," I call out, winding around the table and chasing after her. The house is silent as I walk through the living room and past the sofa, getting a glimpse of a piece she's been working on in the open sketchpad. It's a drawing of me holding my guitar with music notes around me. Below it she wrote, *His mouth warmed my soul.*

My heart does this stupid, very unmanly pitter-patter thing inside my chest, but I smile and take off jogging to my room. I check the closet, under my bed, and then, giving up on my room, I head for my mom's room. I search high and low, but can't find her anywhere, so I look in the bathroom. When I still can't find her, I backtrack to the living room. I'm about ready to step through the doorway and into the kitchen when she jumps out from behind the wall and into the doorway right in front of me, scaring the shit out of me.

I press my hand to my chest as I catch my breath and she laughs as she wraps her legs around me and throws all her weight into me, sending us to the ground. I manage to not smack my head on the floor, but my back does hit it hard.

She lands on top of me, her body falling on mine, and then she quickly pushes up so she's sitting on me with one leg on each side. Her hands come down beside my head as she stares down at me, her hair veiling around our faces.

"That is for all the times you wrestled me to the ground," she says, seeming very pleased with herself as she pants for air.

I shake my head as I sneak my hands to her hips. "Have I taught you nothing?" With one swift movement, I flip us over so she's on the ground and I'm lying on top of her. "I always win at wrestling."

Then I kiss her.

❧

Hours later we're lying in my bed, our bodies tangled together as she lies naked on her side. She hasn't read the journal page yet and I'm not going to push her. Instead she has her sketchbook out and she's scribbling lines down on a fresh sheet of paper, attempting to recapture a photo of her mom sitting on her bed, looking sad. On the other side of the sketchbook there's a picture of what looks like me with the words *My everything* written on the bottom.

"What exactly are you working on?" I ask her as I trace a path up and down her spine, and with each stroke she shivers. "I know this one's your mom"—I tap my finger on the drawing of me—"but what's this one about?"

The pencil briefly stops moving across the paper. "Can I explain it to you later?" She peers over her shoulder and wisps of her hair fall into her face. "I want to finish it first and then tell you everything."

Everything. What does she mean by "everything"? "Can I have a hint?"

She studies me, chewing on her lip, and then she directs her attention back down at the drawing, covered with angled lines and dark shades. "It's about our past...and our future."

Our future. I'm surprised by her honesty and feel guilty because she's been so honest with me lately and I've been keeping a huge secret from her. Well, not exactly a secret, but I've been withholding information, concerned about how she'll react, fearing she'll say she'll go even though she doesn't want to. Or she'll say she won't go and that will be the end of my music dream. But it's time to stop avoiding the decision, especially when she's being so straightforward.

I let my finger trail up her back a few more times and then I drape my arm over her side and press my face against the back of her neck, folding my arms around her. "I have to tell you something," I say, and her body goes as rigid as a board. "Calm down. It's not bad. It's just news...a decision we need to make."

I hear her drop the pen onto the paper. "Okay." She sounds anxious.

I kiss the back of her neck and shut my eyes. "I got a call from Mike the other day."

"Oh, yeah? What'd he want?" She's trying to act calm but I can tell she isn't.

I open my eyes and press my cheek against her skin. "You remember that Rocking Slam Tour that I was telling you about a while ago?"

"The tour you really wanted to go on but didn't think you were good enough to get on?" She rotates over onto her back and looks at me. "The one with all the bands and singers who you idolize?"

"Yeah, that's the one."

She pauses. "Did you get on?"

I nod slowly. "I did."

A smile gradually rises on her face. "I'm so happy for you." She smashes a cheerful kiss against my lips, shocking me, and I'm too surprised to even kiss her back. When she pulls away, she looks confused as she assesses my reaction. "What's wrong? Why aren't you happy about this?"

"Because…" I trail off, searching for the right words. Finally, I sit up and bring one of my knees up, resting my elbow on top of it. "The tour starts in a few weeks and goes for a few months."

She sits up and hugs her knees against her bare chest, trying to look okay about it but sadness fills her eyes. "So you'd be gone for a few months?"

I nod, staring out the window at the glow of the Christmas lights shining against the ice on the house. "And I'd have to cancel our honeymoon."

She presses her lips together, like she wants to say something, but she's trying to fight it. Then she lowers her head onto her knees. "I don't care about the honeymoon. I want you to live out your dream."

I'm silent for a moment as I work to pick up on her vibe, the real one that she's trying to hide from me. "Pretty girl, tell me what you're thinking?" I ask, because I can't read her very well at the moment.

"I'm thinking you should go," she says, lifting her head up. "I'm not going to hold you back. I promised myself I'd never do that."

"You wouldn't be holding me back." I scoot closer to her and put a leg on each side of her. "I want to be with you no matter what."

"I know you do," she says, taking my hands in hers. "And you will. We'll just be apart for three months, which we've done many times."

"And I was miserable all those times." I pull my hands back only to put them on her legs so I can spread them open. "I don't think I should go." I pull her toward me and wrap her long legs around me, feeling a ping of disappointment, but knowing it's right. If she's not going, than neither am I.

"No, you're going to go and you're going to love it. I'm not going to have it any other way." She looks me straight in the eyes like she means business. "I won't marry you if you don't."

I don't know what to say. I know her well enough that I know she's probably not one hundred percent okay with this, but she's trying to make me happy. But I don't want to go without her.

"Come with me," I sputter out abruptly, sounding like an idiot.

Her eyes widen. "On the road for three months?"

I nod, getting a little excited at my sporadic, yet brilliant idea. "It could be fun. You and me and the car and the road. It could be our first adventure as husband and wife. We always said we'd go places when we were kids. In fact, we promised one day we would. This could be our chance."

"For three months?" she repeats. "That's a long time on the road and I have school and work."

"You could take a break from work and take online classes maybe," I suggest and then feel like an ass for even asking her to do such a thing.

She gets quiet, thinking about what I said, looking panicked and lost and excited all at the same time.

"You don't have to decide now," I tell her, not wanting her to feel pressure to do something she doesn't want to do. "Just think about it for a few days."

She hesitates and then conclusively nods. "All right, I'll think about it, but only if you do one thing for me."

"Anything."

A slow grin spans across her face. "Play me the song."

253

Chapter Twenty

Ella

Go on the road for three months with him? Really? It's crazy to even think about, yet at the same time I want to go. It's not like I'd truly miss my job at the art gallery and I could finish school online. In fact, the more I think about it, the more I wonder why I'm even thinking about it at all. I should just go with him. Live life to the fullest. Draw. Be happy. Relax. I've never done that before, never thought I could. But suddenly it hits me: I can. Holy crap. I could just do whatever I want. Travel on the road with him, listening to him play, watching him up on stage as his words move me the way he always does whenever he sings. It seems so damn easy, so why am I hesitating?

I decide after he plays me his song I'll tell him that I'll go with him. That way he won't have to worry about leaving me behind, because I know he is. *Oh my God, I'm seriously going to do this.*

254

Dressed in only his boxers, Micha gets his guitar from the closet and sits down at the foot of the bed. Holding the guitar in his lap, he wraps his long arms around it, and then plucks at the strings. "You know, I'm sort of nervous." His eyes skim over my body as I relax against the wall with only a sheet draped over my naked body. "I never in a million years imagined you'd be naked when I played you this."

I can't help but smile as I fluff up a pillow and lean against it. "You know, I'm not going to even be surprised if somewhere in your song you talk about me being naked."

"No way." He lowers his head, his blond hair hanging down into his aqua eyes as he positions the guitar. "This song was not about my horny feelings for you. Only about my love." He peers up, grinning, but it's underlined with nervousness.

I roll my eyes, but my stomach flutters. "So sappy."

He wiggles his eyebrows at me and then he grows silent, holding his breath. "Are you ready for this, Ella May? Because it's super intense."

I nod excitedly. "Bring on the intensity."

His fingers start moving gracefully across the strings, and everything around me, the room, my thoughts, my body blurs away into something that I never thought I could be. When he sings the first few lyrics, the soft, melodious sound of his voice blankets me and I float away to a place of memories linked to emotions that connect his soul to mine.

> *I see you standing inside the crowd, heart*
> *hidden inside, drowning in pain, no way*
> *to get out.*
> *The pain stabs at my heart, bleeds inside me,*
> *because if you'd just let me, I'd take all the*
> *pain away.*
> *You think no one needs you. That you don't*
> *deserve anything else, so you let yourself*
> *drown.*
> *But I sink with you, refusing to let go. I want to*
> *take away the pain and let it bleed into*
> *my soul.*

He starts to pluck the strings with more passion, the volume increasing as he closes his eyes, his voice intensifying as he reaches the chorus.

> *Know that no matter what happens*
> *through the hurt, the sadness, the burning ache*
> *inside my chest*
> *I'll always be with you, inside and out.*

> *Through hard times and helpless ones, through*
> *love, through doubt*
> *My heart is yours forever. I'll never let go. I'll never*
> *let you sink.*
> *I'll carry your pain for you if you just let me.*

He pauses as he plays a few more intense notes and then opens his lips again.

> *The way I feel about you burns deep inside*
> *my chest, feelings I hold in, but desperately*
> *want to let out.*
> *It hurts every time I'm around you, hoping things*
> *will change, that somehow I'll find a way to*
> *save you,*
> *find a way to stop you from drowning, pull you*
> *back and take your place, let the pain take*
> *me over.*
> *God, please just let me take the pain away before*
> *it kills me because I can't watch you drown*
> *anymore.*
> *Because I need you. I want you. I can't live*
> *without you.*

The pitch of his voice is a little uneven at the end,

but it still sounds beautiful and his fingers keep playing, his eyes still shut.

Know that no matter what happens
through the hurt, the sadness, the burning ache
        inside my chest
I'll always be with you, inside and out.
Through hard times and helpless ones, through
        love, through doubt
my heart is yours forever. I'll never let go. I'll never
        let you sink.
I'll carry your pain if you just let me.
God, please just let me.

His voice drifts off as he plucks a sequence of notes and then finishes the song. He sits quietly for a moment, his chest rising and falling before he opens his eyes. Then he takes one look at me and his eyes widen in alarm.

"Shit." He shoves the guitar aside and scoots across the bed toward me. "Baby, you don't need to cry. It wasn't supposed to be a sad song."

I touch my fingers to my cheeks and they're soaked with tears. I hadn't even realized I was crying, but I'm guessing I probably began from the start because each word hit me powerfully in the heart.

"I'm not sad," I tell him, wiping the tears away with my hand. "I just didn't know you felt like that all the way back when you were fifteen. It means you felt like that for a really long time."

He traces his fingers down my cheeks, erasing the tears, but the feelings behind them still linger in me and I'm glad. "I couldn't even understand the lyrics myself at first, but when I finally did I realized I loved you and I'd do anything to make you happy."

More tears flow from me and I don't even try to hold them back—I couldn't even if I tried. Too much emotion was in that song and it still burns in my heart, too fresh, raw, but in the most wonderfully real way. I think about all those years when it was just him and me and the many more years we have ahead of us.

As I climb onto his lap, I circle my arms around him and hug him tightly. "Just so you know, you were the one who didn't let me drown. If it weren't for you, I probably would have given up," I say and he rubs his hand up and down my back. "And I'm glad you didn't let me."

Chapter Twenty-One

Micha

I wasn't expecting her to cry. I knew the song was really intense and emotional, which is why I'd never sung it to anyone before, but Ella's not a crier and her tears only added beauty to the moment.

I hold on to her as the sun disappears behind the mountains and the room shifts to a dark gray, the lamp the only source of light in the room. Finally her tears subside and she moves away from my chest. Her eyes are red and puffy as she dabs her fingers across her cheeks. "So what did you find in my mom's journal?" she asks.

I raise my eyebrows. "You want to read it now? I thought you wanted to wait?"

She brushes her hair out of her face. "I guess so, since you said I had to read them before the wedding and it's tomorrow."

I smile as she traces the cursive lines of the tattoo on my rib cage. "Tomorrow and you're all mine."

Her lips itch to smile as she stares down at the tattoo. "I think I was yours a long time ago."

"You think so?"

"No, I know so, at least I do now." She tilts to the side and grabs the journal off my nightstand and then hands it to me. "Will you read it to me…the page you said I need to read?"

I nervously nod, hoping she'll take what I read as a good thing, and then I lie us down on our sides, facing each other with our heads on the pillow and our legs tangled together underneath the sheet. Her fingers fold around my ribs as I hold the journal up, turning it to the page that I marked. "I think it's the vows she wrote right before she married your dad."

"Really?" She seems shocked. "Are you sure they're her vows, because it didn't seem like she was too eager to marry him."

"Well, I'm pretty sure this is about your dad, since it says *To Raymond* on the top," I say with a smile. "And it's nice, what she wrote. Short and simple, but nice."

"Is that how our vows are going to be?" she asks, peeking up through her long lashes, giving me a hopeful look.

"They can be however you want them to be," I reply. "And if you still want to back out, you can."

"No, thanks." She nestles her head into the crook of my shoulder. "'K, I'm ready. Read what she wrote."

I take a deep breath.

I was living in a world where nothing made sense. Darkness. Instability. Life on the verge of death. Then you came into my life and shined through the darkness, showing me that light did exist. And for a moment I walked the path, breathed for the first time in a long time. You gave me air and I wouldn't have it any other way. Without you, I wouldn't remember what it was like not to suffocate. Without you, I wouldn't remember what the light felt like. And I'll always love you for that, Raymond Daniels.

I stop reading and look down at Ella, checking her reaction. She looks like she's going to cry again and then suddenly she sits up and moves out of my arms.

Before I can respond, she's climbing out of bed and pulling a shirt over her head.

"What are you doing?" I ask, sitting up.

She slips on a pair of jeans, shimmying them up

to her hips, and then she fastens the button. "Going to talk to my dad."

I'm puzzled, but I don't want to press. She doesn't look upset, only eager as she puts on her boots and reaches for her jacket hanging on the bedpost. Then she takes the journal from me, rips out the page I just read, and stuffs it into her pocket.

"I'm going to give this to my dad." She leans across the bed and presses her lips to my mouth. "I'll be right back," she says, breathless with enthusiasm as she hurries to the door, leaving me alone in my room and a little stunned.

I wasn't expecting her to be so enthusiastic about it, but I'm glad she is. I want her to be happy. I just hope I can keep doing that for her, make all the right decisions, keep her smiling, laughing, keep any pain away, just like my lyrics begged her to let me do.

Chapter Twenty~Two

Ella

I run over to my house with a crazy amount of energy fueled by the piece of paper in my pocket. I'm not even sure if it is her vows. In fact, I think it's not, but what I do know is that my dad deserves to read the words, deserves to know that at one time he made my mom happy when it seemed like it was impossible.

The Firebird is parked in the driveway, so I know my dad's home. When I burst into the kitchen, I'm relieved to find he's eating dinner at the table and he's alone.

He still has on his work clothes, a stained white shirt and jeans that are specked with red paint and there's some paint splattered on his hands. He has a plate with chicken, potatoes, and a roll on it and a cup of milk in front of him.

His head snaps up in my direction as I come barreling inside the house. "Ella, what's wrong?" he asks, pushing away from the table and getting to his feet. "You look upset."

"No, I'm fine. I promise," I say, breathless as I take the piece of paper out of my pocket. "In fact, I'm sort of happy right now."

"Well, I'm glad." His face contorts with confusion, as he looks down at the paper in my outstretched hand. "What is that?"

"It was in Mom's journal," I say and his face falls and his mouth plummets to a frown. "Just take it," I insist. "And read it. I promise you won't regret it."

He hesitates and then takes the paper from me. His fingers tremble as he unfolds it and smoothes out the creases. His eyes start to skim the paper. Seconds tick by and tears form in the corners of his eyes. The tremble in his hands intensifies the farther down he gets and I can tell he's about to cry, but not out of pain. He doesn't look upset or hurt. Or disappointed. Or sad. He looks...well, strangely relieved.

When he's finished, he carefully folds it up and then holds it in his hand like it's something precious. "You said you got this out of her journal?" he asks as he looks up at me.

I nod as I wrap my coat tightly around myself, hoping he's feeling at least a little happiness knowing he made Mom happy. "It was the last page. Was it…was it her vows for your wedding?"

He shakes his head as he stares at the paper in his hand, a tear or two dripping of his eyes. I'm not sure if I've ever seen him cry before and witnessing it seems like some sort of miracle that makes me happy but also a little uncomfortable.

He breathes in and out for several minutes and then he collects himself and pats my shoulder, giving me this strange look before he pulls me in for a very awkward hug. He smells like cigarettes and paint, but there's no scent of booze. It's different and weird, like the hug itself. I remember all those times when I was younger and I watched the other moms at the park hug their kids when they got hurt or just because they wanted to. The many times I watched Micha's mom hug him when she was happy, sad, or when she wanted to say she was sorry. I remember the first time I was hugged. I was eight and I'd scraped my knee open. Micha tried to hug me better like his mom did with him. His arms barely made it around me before I freaked out and shoved him to the ground. I think about all the hugs that came after that, though, and how each of them became easier.

This one with my dad is far from easy, but maybe if we do it more often, it'll become easier, just like moving forward in my life has become.

❧

When I get back to Micha's house, it's past nine o'clock. The air is deathly cold and seeping into the quiet house. I kick my boots off at the back door, hang up my jacket on the coatrack, and then pad through the kitchen to Micha's bedroom, only to find the room dark and him asleep in the bed, his face snuggled into the pillow with the blanket over him.

I flip the lamp on, slip my jeans off, and then quickly hop under the blanket with him. He stirs as I nuzzle up to him, then tenses when my chilled skin touches his.

"Are you awake?" I ask as I comb my fingers through his soft hair.

He lets out a sigh as his hands find my hips beneath the blanket. "I was having such a good dream, where you snuck into my room and started touching me, but not my hair. It was a much lower place. I think you should try to find it."

I smile as my fingers drift down his firm chest. "I have to tell you something."

He eyes open, and they're red and full of sleepiness. "Should I be worried?"

I shake my head. "Not at all."

He slides an arm over my stomach and pulls me closer to him. "Tell me then."

"I want to go on the road with you," I say and as soon as I say it, I know it's the right choice. For us. "I'll take the rest of my classes online and quit my job."

He's silent and full of surprise. It takes him a moment to answer and when he speaks his voice is off pitch. "Are you sure you want to quit your job?"

"I want to be with you all the time. And I want to watch you play and just draw things that mean stuff to me, like you and I and the places we've been, all our spots, like the lake and your room, the tree you used to climb to get into my window...the one that always brought you to me," I say with honesty. "If I could picture my life being any way, that's how I'd picture it. It's what I want to do."

His expression is unreadable as he searches my eyes for the truth. "Are you sure? Because you have a few weeks to think about it and I want you to be absolutely sure. I never want you to do anything you don't want to do. I—"

I interrupt him. "Micha, I'm sure if you're sure. I want to spend as much time as I can with you—I want to be with you and I want you to live out your dream."

"I'm sure about anything as long as it means I get

to have you," he tells me with passion in his tone as he shakes his head with bewilderment in his eyes, like he can't believe that this is happening. "And yes, I want you to come with me more than anything."

"Even more than you want to marry me?"

"Maybe not quite that much, but it's close."

We share a quiet moment as we contemplate our future and where it'll hopefully take us. At least that's what I'm thinking about. With Micha, I never know, especially when his hand wanders down to my ass and he gets this naughty look on his face.

"Are you nervous about tomorrow?" he asks as he presses his mouth against my forehead. His finger circles around the infinity mark on my lower back, sending shivers and tickling vibrations through my body.

"Honestly, yeah," I tell him as my fingers hook the top of his boxers. "You?"

He slides his hand up my side and then down my arm to my hand. "Honestly, a little, but mainly because I'm worried everyone's going to freeze their asses off."

"Are you nervous that I'll run?" I don't even know why I ask it. It just sort of slips out and I can't help but think of the morning after the night on the bridge, when I decided to run and then just a week ago when we were originally supposed to get married. Neither time was because I didn't love him. Even the night on the bridge, I did love him even though I wouldn't admit it. And that time I ran because I didn't love myself.

"Honestly?" he asks and I nod. "No, not really."

"Not at all?" I ask. "Even considering my past?"

He shakes his head. "I know that you love me, Ella May. Just like I know that emotions freak you out, but deep down you feel more about us than a lot of people feel in their lifetime. Just like I know that you're scared and excited at the same time. Just like I know that every single day I've spent with you, good and bad, has been worth it. And it's because of those things that I know that you'll walk up that aisle that Lila's going to make you walk up, say your vows, kiss me, and then we'll have our happy, sad, sometimes-good, sometimes-bad, crazy, bumpy, intense, worth-the-journey ever after."

His words plunge into my heart and tears well up in my eyes again. "Are you going to say that in your vows tomorrow, because it was pretty perfect."

He smiles against my forehead. "No, I have something better planned for tomorrow."

I lean back and look him in the eyes, which are sparkling. "Oh yeah?"

"Yes, yeah." He lowers his mouth toward mine. "And it's even better than the lyrics." And then he kisses me as his hands explore my body. By the time we pull away, we're exhausted, naked, and sweaty and it's just after midnight.

"Hey," I tell Micha as I look at the clock. "It's officially our wedding day and Christmas."

"Are you ready to go through with this?" Micha asks as he pins me between his legs and arms.

I nod with my eyes closed, but my heart is knocking inside my chest, wanting to flee. I'm going to get married today. *Holy shit!* "Yeah."

"You sound nervous," he remarks, kissing the top of each of my eyelids.

"I am," I admit. "But that's probably normal, right?"

"I'm sure it is."

"Are you nervous?"

He hesitates. "Yeah, a little."

I free a breath trapped in my chest and open my eyes. "I'm glad."

"That I'm nervous?" he questions.

I nod, sliding one of my legs out from between his and hitching it over his hip. "Because it means we're on the same page and usually that's not the case."

He considers what I said and then bends his knee so it's pressed up between my legs, his body heat blissfully scorching against my skin. "I guess you could look at it that way, at least if it'll get you up the aisle."

"I'll be fine," I assure him, cringing at the idea of

either walking up the aisle alone or with my dad. Neither seems that appealing because alone I'm probably going to freak out, and with my dad, if I do freak out, he won't be able to calm me down. "Micha...will you...will you walk up the aisle with me or tell Lila we're just going to skip that part?"

"Can't you just tell her?" he asks, frowning.

I shake my head. "She's wedding crazy. Seriously, I think she should consider becoming a wedding planner."

His arms slip around my waist and then he tastes my mouth with his tongue. "If you want me to walk up the aisle with you, then I will."

"Thank you," I whisper and hug him tightly, knowing that if he's there with me it'll be so much easier to get through it. Everything is when he's with me.

It's quiet for a while, and when Micha speaks again, he sounds a little bit excited.

"So since it's officially Christmas," Micha says pulling away from me slightly to look me in the eye, "are you going to give me my Christmas present?"

I frown. "It's a really silly present."

"So what?" he says. "Besides, silly presents are the best."

I sigh and then sit up, slipping from his hold, and pad over to my duffel bag that's on the floor in front of the bed. "Okay, but try not to get too disappointed when you open it," I say, taking out the wrapped-up box with a bow on it. I climb back in to bed and hand it to him.

He grins at the box as he crisscrosses his legs. "Aw, you even wrapped it and put a bow on it and everything," he says in a teasing voice.

I shake my head and playfully pinch his arm. "Don't make fun of me. And Lila made me wrap it."

"I like that you wrapped it," he says and then rips off the paper like a little kid would. I put the bracelets into a small box, so he has to open that as well. When he gets the lid off, he stares at the thin strips of leather with the words *forever* engraved on both of them.

When he doesn't say anything, I start to grow nervous, like he might not get what they are. "They're like the ones we used to have when we were kids, but I didn't get the one that says 'best friends,' figuring since we are way more than that I'd just get two forevers."

He glances up at me and I can't read his expression at all. "I remember. You actually made me wear the one that said 'best friends' and it made me sort of feel girly."

I frown, regretting the present. "Yet you still wore it."

"Because you asked me to," he says. "And we both know I'd do anything for you."

"Sorry, it's sappy, right?" I reach for the box to take the bracelets back. "I should have gotten you something better."

He quickly picks up the box and turns, holding it out of my reach. "Are you kidding me? This is perfect."

"But you just said they were girly."

"No, I said that having a bracelet that said 'best friends' was girly and that was when I was eight." He smiles and I start to relax as he takes out one of the bracelets. "This is the perfect present, Ella May, because it means something."

"It's kind of a sappy present though," I say as he slips the bracelet on.

"Which makes you a sap, just like me," he replies as he takes my wrist and slips the other bracelet on.

"I guess you must be wearing on me," I joke, and then lean in to kiss him. "But that's okay." I fiddle with the bracelet, reducing the size so it'll fit my wrist, while Micha gets out of bed and starts digging through his dresser drawer. I think he's looking for a shirt to put on or something, since it's freezing, so I'm surprised when he returns to the bed still shirtless but with a small wooden box in his hand.

"Now, I didn't have time to wrap it since I got it for you tonight," he says, handing the box to me, his hand shaking a little bit, like it did last Christmas when he gave me the engagement ring. "Merry Christmas, Ella May-soon-to-be Scott."

I smile, but I'm a little nervous at what the hell he could be giving me that would make him nervous. I take a deep breath as I open the box. Inside is a ribbon necklace with a rose pendant.

"It's beautiful," I say with honesty as I run my fingers along the pendant, which feels like porcelain.

Micha lets out a loud breath as he scoots closer to me. "It's actually from me and your father. It belonged to your mother. He gave it to her on their wedding day and we sort of thought maybe you could wear it at our wedding, as a way to sort of be close to her."

It's like he's pushed this button and without warning I start to cry, tears streaming down my cheeks like a fountain, dripping down my lips, my nose, onto the necklace in the box. I'm not even a crier, yet for some reason, I seem to be crying a lot lately. Usually, I'd fight them back, but I really don't care at the moment. I just cry. Cry because I'm happy and sad at the same time. Sad because my mom won't be there, but happy because I'm marrying the love of my life tomorrow.

My head tips down so it takes Micha a second to realize I'm crying. When he does, he cups my face and lifts my head back, immediately wiping the tears away with a worried look on his face.

"I'm sorry," he says. "I was worried about giving it to you because I thought it'd upset you."

I press my lips together and shake my head. "I'm not upset at all."

"Then why are you crying?"

"Because I'm happy," I say with a smile as tears continue to pour out.

He still looks unconvinced. "So you like the present?"

"I love the present," I say and then kiss him with so much passion we collapse back onto the bed, the wooden box still clutched in my hand. We kiss until we're breathless, and then I pull away only to say, "The present is perfect—you're perfect."

And he really, really is.

Chapter Twenty-Three

Micha

"Oh my God, you two and your fucking crazy-ass ideas." Ethan paces back and forth, flattening a path in the snow in front of my car with his hands stuffed in the pockets of his jeans, a hoodie pulled over his black button-down shirt. I went for a different look, wearing a pinstriped buttoned shirt Ella picked out for me, black jeans, and boots, along with a dark jacket we borrowed from Thomas. She made me roll up the sleeves and keep my leather bands on my wrists because she said it made me look sexy. Honestly, I don't really give a shit what I'm wearing just as long as she's happy.

"What?" I ask, popping the trunk of the Chevelle. The snow was so deep driving up that I had to put chains on the tires and it was still a pain in the ass to get down here, so I'm a little worried about going back. "It's just a little cold air."

He shakes his head as he glares at me. "We're all going to be ice statues by the time this is over, buried alive under five feet of snow."

"Hey, we'll make great snowmen," I joke as I glance up at the sky where light, fluffy snowflakes drift toward the ground, landing in the bare branches of the trees and covering the ice-covered lake. Lila came down here a little earlier with my mom and scattered candles around a flattened-out area in snow beneath a canopy of trees, although I have no idea how the hell they're going to get them lit. They also tied black and red ribbons all over the branches along with silvery Christmas lights that are plugged into an extension cord that's plugged into an AC adapter in my car, which means I have to leave the engine on for the entire wedding. They sprinkled rose petals all over the snow, which I can barely see now because of the fresh layer of snowflakes on top of them. After they did all this, they took off to go check on Ella and help her get ready. I'm glad she's not alone, because she seemed a little nervous when I left the house.

As I unload a few fold-up chairs from the trunk, I pretend I'm not nervous, even though I am. Not because I want to bail but because I'm fucking getting married and it's starting to freak me out. Ethan's responsibility lecture is fresh in my mind and I keep thinking, What if I screw up? I can't. Not with Ella.

"You okay, man?" Ethan asks, dropping a few chairs onto a growing pile. "You look a little pale."

"I'm fine." I put my foot on the bottom bar of a chair and stomp down on it to unfold it, and then I stand it up in the snow.

"Make sure you line them up straight," Ethan says as he unfolds a chair and lines it up with the one I just set up. "Lila will chew our asses out if we don't."

I smile, but keep my head down as I start forming an even row. It doesn't take more than a minute to get the few chairs set up, since there's hardly anyone attending the wedding, but it seems like an eternity goes by. By the time we're done, I'm fidgety and jittery, a bundle of nerves sparking inside me.

Finally I can't take it anymore. Adrenaline is rushing through me and my pulse is erratic so I go back to my Chevelle and open the glove box. Digging around beneath a stack of papers, I find a pack of cigarettes that I hid in there ages ago for moments just like these.

"Really?" Ethan questions as I sit down in the driver's seat with the door open and my feet planted in the snow.

"I just need to calm down," I say and pop one into my mouth. He shakes his head, laughing under his breath as I grab the lighter out of the pack, cup my hand around the end of the cigarette, and light it. As soon as the nicotine enters my lungs, I feel better and my heart rate starts to settle.

Ethan heaves a large Tupperware bin out of the trunk and drops it onto the ground as I suck drag after drag off the cigarette, my heart calming, my skin warming under my coat and shirt.

"You feel better?" he asks as I graze my thumb over the end of the cigarette and scatter ash across the snow.

I savor another breath of smoke. "Actually, I do."

He rolls his eyes. Ethan never did like it when I smoked, except I think he used to smoke pot. He would always chew me out, though, for getting ash in his truck and stinking up the upholstery.

After I finish the cigarette I put it out in the snow as a large maroon SUV comes bumping down the road. I wish I had some cologne on hand because now I stink and Ella's going to know I've been smoking. She won't get mad at me, but she knows I do it when something's wrong, and knowing her, she'll think it's because I don't want to get married.

The SUV stops close to the Chevelle and the engine keeps running as Dean hops out, zipping up his coat. His hair is combed to the side and he has these really shiny shoes on. I remember when we were younger, how he had an eyebrow piercing and was obsessed with the idea that one day he would have tattoos all over his arms and a goatee.

"Hey, man, you might want to go back to the house and check on Ella," he says, stuffing his hands into the pocket of his slacks as he walks up to me.

I meet him at the front of the car and sit down on the frosted hood, folding my arms. "She said she was going to drive down here with my mom and Lila."

He shakes his head and hitches his thumb over his shoulder, pointing at the road. "She was...is, but something sort of happened."

I stand up, my pulse immediately accelerating as the fear that I've been stood up again races through my mind. "Why? What happened?"

He looks tense and uncomfortable, rocking back on his heels. "I'm not really sure. All I know is that Ella's friend...that blonde girl, told me I should probably come get you."

I don't even wait for him to say anything else. I get inside the car, unplug the lights, and press on the gas, hoping it's not what I'm thinking.

Hoping she's not standing me up again.

Chapter Twenty~Four

Ella

Breathe.

Breathe.

Breathe.

I'm trying to get air into my lungs, but I feel like I'm suffocating, invisible fingers wrapping around my neck as I battle for oxygen. I don't even know where the panic attack stemmed from. One minute I was fine, getting my hair pinned up as I listened to Lila talk about her and Ethan's road trip plans and the next I felt like I was drowning in the fact that as soon as Lila was finished with my hair, I was going to have to put the dress on. Then it'd be time to go to *my wedding*, say my vows, start my future.

I'd flipped out and started bawling, scaring the crap out of Micha's mom, Lila, and Caroline as I jumped out of the chair and raced back into Micha's room. Lila came to check on me as I was bawling on the bed. She tried to talk to me, but I couldn't stop crying. Then I'd pulled a blanket over my head, ready to shut down, but then I'd remembered all the progress I'd made over the last couple of years and instead I ended up saying something that shocked me.

"Go get Micha, please." My voice cracks through my sobs.

Lila pauses. "Um, okay." Seconds later, I'd heard the door shut.

After she leaves, I cry for what seems like hours, ruining my makeup as tears stream down my face. I keep trying to tell myself to get out of the damn bed and go put the dress on because deep down I know I want to and I'm just scared. Finally, the door creaks open and I freeze as I hear the soft sound of footsteps padding over to the bed. The mattress sinks as someone sits down on the edge of the bed, and then a hand touches my shoulder on the outside of the blanket.

"Ella…" Micha's voice is alarmingly off pitch. "What's wrong?"

When I don't respond, he pulls the blanket off my head and the cold air stings my skin. I peer up at him through tear-filled eyes and he sighs, looking like he's on the brink of crying too. "Are you…" He swallows hard as he touches my cheek with his fingers, and then he shuts his eyes. "Are you getting cold feet again?"

I shake my head and sit up, rubbing the back of my hand across my face, making my makeup worse, I'm sure. "No, it's not that…I'm just…" I search for what I'm really feeling, because I want to tell him the truth. "I'm just scared. I keep thinking about putting the dress on, walking down the aisle, saying my vows…moving forward. I'm overwhelmed and I needed someone here who got me. Who could help me put my dress on and get me through this." A slow breath eases from my lips as I realize that that's all I want—Micha by my side because he'll get me through this. Sure, I know that sometimes I have to do things on my own, but at the same time admitting when I do need someone makes me stronger.

He opens his eyes and blinks back the tears. "Are you sure that's it?"

"Yes, I'm sure," I tell him, wholeheartedly. "I just panicked and I'm so sorry. I just need you here with me right now."

He studies me for what feels like forever and then he suddenly slides me to the side of the bed, takes my hand, and pulls me to my feet with this intense look on his face. Releasing my hand, he grabs the bottom of my shirt and tugs it over my head, moving carefully to avoid ruining the curls and braids or knocking out any of the black flowers. He discards my shirt on the floor, and then unties the drawstring of my pajamas, his eyes locked on me as he slips them down my legs. I refuse to look away from him and the longer I focus on him, the calmer I get inside, the violent rainstorm settling into a light drizzle. When the pants reach my feet, I step out of them. He makes his way to the closet and gets my wedding dress. It's a beautiful dress, a shimmering black silk top, a red ribbon securing the back, and an elegant flowing white bottom bunched together in places by red and black roses.

Micha slips the plastic straps off the hanger as he returns to me and then lowers the dress to the floor so I can step into it. Once I get my legs through, he guides the fabric up my body until the top covers my breasts. Then I hold the front up with one hand and he walks behind me and grazes his fingers down my spine.

"Feeling any better?" he asks, his breath hot on my neck and I shiver.

I nod, freeing a trapped breath. "A lot better actually."

"Good, because I want you to feel better. I want you to feel good about this—about marrying me, Ella May." He slowly zips up the dress and the fabric constricts against my body, pushing my breasts up the slightest bit. Once he gets it zipped, he steps back in front of me, nudging the flowing bottom out of the way with his boot. "Are you sure you want this—want me forever?" He has this guarded look in his eyes, like he's trying to pretend that he can handle whatever, but I can tell that if I say no—that I don't want this—it'll crush him.

"Micha, I want this more than I've ever wanted anything," I say honestly as I run my fingers along the bottom of my eyes and across my cheeks. "Just let me fix my makeup and we can go. I'm sure I look hideous."

"You look beautiful," he says without missing a beat. "You always do."

"Hideously beautiful, I think you mean," I joke, and he cracks a smile, his fingers seeking my cheek.

"No, you look beautiful," he promises. "But if you want to fix your makeup you can. I don't think I can do that for you."

I smile and pick up my makeup bag from the dresser, but he ends up holding one of my hands so it's sort of like he's helping me, only it makes the actual act of putting makeup on a bit complicated. But I manage and I end up getting the black eyeliner and lip gloss on without any mishaps. When I'm done, I sit on my bed and Micha kneels down in front of me and helps me put on my boots.

"I feel like Cinderella," I remark as I put my foot in and he laces the boot up.

He peers up at me and a smile touches his lips. "Good. That's how you should feel." He stands up and then guides me to my feet before he leans in to kiss me. Then he walks over to the nightstand and picks up the wooden box he gave me last night. He opens it up, takes out the necklace, and, stepping behind me, puts it on me. As soon as the ribbon and rose are secured around my neck, I feel weirdly at peace.

He kisses the back of my neck and then walks around in front of me. "Are you ready for this?" His tone's light but I can tell he's worried about my response.

"I'm more than ready," I tell him and then grab the front of his shirt and pull him in for another kiss. When I pull away, I give him a questioning look. "Wait a minute…did you smoke?"

He scratches the back of his neck, looking guilty. "Sort of, but only because I was a little nervous."

"About what?"

"About starting our future…taking care of you the right way. I just want to make you happy."

"You have since the day we became friends," I assure him and the anxious look in his eyes evaporates as I slip on my leather jacket and tuck the photo of my mom inside it because I want her with me, even if it is just a picture.

He gives me a funny look, but he doesn't say anything and then we leave the room, holding hands, and head to our wedding together and everything feels right because he's here by my side and I wouldn't have it any other way.

Chapter Twenty~Five

Micha

She looks beautiful in her dress, her hair all done up in braids and curls, her green eyes big as she stares at me, gripping onto my hands for dear life as we get out of the car. I try to stay calm but my hammering pulse makes it hard to breathe, not because I'm nervous but because I'm excited. I turn on "The Story," by Brandi Carlile, so it's quietly playing through the speakers, and Ella smiles, remembering how it was playing at Dean and Caroline's wedding when I told her that I wanted to marry her.

"You remembered the song," she says.

"Of course I did," I reply, extending my elbow to her. "It was an epic moment in our history."

She loops her arm through mine and then we start to walk up to the aisle. By the time we make it up the snowy rose-covered path, with our friends and family staring at us, I feel so content and happy, knowing that in a few moments Ella will be mine forever and I'll be hers. I think a few of them are a little bit surprised to see this actually taking place, particularly Ethan and Lila, who are cuddled up together and who look a little bit shocked when we get out of the car. My mom, however, looks like she's been pretty much waiting for this day. She nearly beams as she sits with Thomas, watching us with more happiness in her eyes than I've ever seen. Dean looks neutral, just how he always looks, and Caroline's almost in tears. And Ella's dad's a little harder to read, but it almost looks like he's about to tear up.

At the end, we stand under the canopy of the trees as the minister starts reading a marriage speech that I barely pay attention to. Snowflakes dot Ella's hair and melt against her chest where the rose pendant rests just above her breasts, making her skin wet. She looks perfect and I seriously want to lick her right now, but I don't think it would be appropriate, so I tell myself to keep cool until later tonight when I can do anything I want to her.

I basically zone out and focus on her until the minister announces it's time for me to read my vows. Then I let go of Ella's hand only to take out the folded-up piece of paper from my pocket, my fingers shaking as I unfold it.

Ella looks nervous, her breath increasing and causing more haze to surround her face as she waits to hear what I have to say, the truth about how I feel about her.

"I can't think of a time when I didn't want to be with you." I glance back and forth between the paper and her as I speak. "From the moment you stepped out the door of your house, I thought you were beautiful and I wanted you in my life. I can't say it was love at first sight since I was too young and I don't believe in love at first sight. I believe in finding the right person who makes everything easy, who makes me happy, who makes life worth living and more exciting, whether it's kissing on swing sets," I say and that gets her to smile, "racing cars, getting tattoos, sharing Popsicles and tears, or just sitting in my room singing while you draw. I couldn't have done life without you and every single moment, good or bad, has been worth it because it got us right here to this very place and this very moment where I get to have you for the rest of my life. You make me happier than I can even begin to explain. I love you, Ella May, more than life itself, and I'll continue to love you until I take my last breath—I'll love you forever. You own my heart." By the end, my voice is getting unsteady with the emotions flooding through me as I think about everything we've gone through to get to this place and that in a few moments she will be mine forever, the girl next door who I fell in love with and gave my heart to completely.

I suck in an uneven breath as I stuff the paper back in my pocket, knowing Ethan's going to tease the shit out of me for acting so emotional, but at the moment I don't care.

I keep my attention on Ella, watching her as she fights tears back and takes a piece of paper out of her jacket pocket.

She stares at it for an eternity, like she can't find her voice, and her hands tremble. My heart constricts in my chest as I wait for her to say what I mean to her, worried she won't be able to do it. But then, surprising me, she finally releases a deafening breath and the sound of her voice sends a rush of relief through me.

"You know, when I first met you, you scared the shit out of me." She pulls a "whoops" face and glances at the minister, who sighs because he knows us well enough to know this is just how we talk. Then she returns her focus to me and clears her throat. "You were so intense and determined to get to know me and I couldn't understand why you would want to, for a lot of reasons, reasons that you know about because you know me better than anyone." Her voice wobbles a little and she lets go of the paper and wipes her sweaty palm on her jacket. "But eventually you sort of wore on me." Her lips quirk and it makes me grin. "You became my light in my dark life and you made me feel so loved that I'd forget how to breathe. You were the only one who could make me laugh, smile, have fun, not give up. You were always there for me and somehow, through the crazy, intense years, you fought your way into my soul and ended up becoming my everything. You became my lifeline, the one person I could rely on no matter what, whether I was upset or pushing you away—you were always there for me. And I love you for it and for the amazing person that you are, for writing me songs and tattooing them on your skin, for wearing a ridiculous O-ring on your finger," she says, trying to smile but I can tell she's getting overwhelmed by her emotions. "And for loving me enough not to let me give up, no matter how hard I fought." A breath gradually eases from her lips as she stuffs the paper into her jacket pocket.

When she looks up at me, tears are forming in her eyes. She's overwhelmed with emotion and I'm sure she can see the same emotion mirrored in my face. I've never seen her be so open like that and I think, if it's even possible, I might have just fallen in love with her more.

It's quiet for a moment as everyone just sort of watches us, and then Ethan lets out a loud cough and I shake my head as Ella rolls her eyes. Lila hisses something at him and then the quietness surrounds us again.

The minister finally continues on to the ring exchange, directing us with what to do. I slip the simple silver wedding band on Ella's finger and her breath falters as she looks down at it and smiles. Then she takes out her ring box and opens it up and it's a silver one that almost matches the one I gave her, only it's a little thicker. She replaces the O-ring with it, her hand shaking as she slips it over my finger.

"I now pronounce you husband and wife," the minister announces and suddenly everything's official. She's my wife and I'm her husband.

I hear someone in the crowd clap their hands as I lean in toward Ella to kiss her. She follows my lead, our lips magnetizing toward each other and we meet halfway. Underneath the trees' branches blanketed with snow, our lips brush and our arms wrap around each other, finally getting to our wonderfully, imperfect, difficult, complex, yet beautiful and worth it, ever after.

Epilogue

Two months later ...

Ella

"Wake up, beautiful," Micha says as he breathes in my ear and presses his warm body up against mine.

"No way," I mutter, burying my face into a pillow as I draw the sheet over my naked body. "I'm too tired."

"Come on, pretty girl. I have a surprise for you." He places a delicate kiss against my neck, slipping his tongue out along my skin before rolling away from me. "Come on, it'll be worth it. I promise." I hear him walk away toward the bathroom. "I'm going to go take a shower. Be ready to go somewhere by the time I get out." Moments later the door shuts and the shower turns on.

I lie in bed for a while, telling myself that I'm not going to get up because I'm too damn tired from all the other mornings he's woken me up this same way.

It's become a tradition. He finds a way to surprise me, whether it's taking me out to breakfast or waking my body up with his tongue.

I finally give in and force myself to open my eyes because I have a hard time saying no to Micha. The sunlight sparkles through the window as I stretch my arms and climb out of bed. I pull a short, black dress out of my suitcase and put it on and then side-braid my hair and secure it with an elastic. After I slip on my sandals, I sink down on the bed and wait for him to get out while I stare at the rings on my fingers. Even two months later, I still can't help but smile when I see them there, marking one of the best days of my life. The day I told Micha how I truly felt, the day he conclusively became mine. We kissed and danced a lot that day, to a list of songs that made an appearance in our history. It was beautiful and magical and really sappy, but all weddings are. Afterward, we spent hours having sex until I felt like my body was going to break apart. It was amazing and exhausting— everything still is amazing and exhausting. And then we packed up our stuff and headed back home to start our life, but not after Micha made us stop by Mikey's house so he could slash his tires, like I promised him he could.

We've been on the road for a little over a month

now and it's been an adventure. Micha was given the option of riding the bus with a few other musicians, but because we missed our honeymoon, he decided that we could at least have a road trip, so we're traveling across the country in the Chevelle, making it our goal to have sex in every state. So far we've gotten up to sixteen, but after tonight it'll be seventeen.

After a while, Micha comes walking out with a towel in his hand, looking gorgeous and sexy in a red plaid shirt that he hasn't buttoned yet so I get a glimpse of his muscles. His jeans ride low on his hips and my body burns as I look at him, thinking about the many times he's used those hips to thrust into me. His hair is wet and flipped at the ends and I bite my lip, wanting to run my fingers through it.

"I'm so happy right now that I think there might be something wrong with me," I divulge and he snorts a laugh as he balls up the towel and tosses it onto the hotel room floor.

"There's nothing wrong with being happy, pretty girl," he says, as he ruffles his blond hair into place. "It's good that you're happy."

"I know that." I stand up and help him button up his shirt while he continues to fuss with his hair. "I hope you are, too, though."

His brows knit as he glances down at me, his aqua

eyes burning with intensity. "Of course I'm happy. You're here with me."

"You know, if your fans knew you talked like that, they'd go even more wild for you."

"No, they'd probably laugh," he says with a shrug. "But I really don't care what they think. Only you."

"Not the female ones." I do up the last button and then link my arms around the back of his neck, standing on my tiptoes. "Okay, where are you taking me today, because I'm dying to know."

"It's a surprise," he says, then grabs my hand and tugs me toward the door.

"You say that every day." I pout as he slips his shoes on.

He grins at me as he picks up my sketchbook and drawing pencil from the dresser. "I know, and that pouty look that you always get on your face when I won't tell you makes it so much fun."

"Why are you grabbing that?" I nod at the sketchbook, closing the door behind us as we step out into the hallway.

"Because you're going to need it," he says, leading me down the hallway.

I sigh and follow him down the stairs and out to the car. We climb in, he starts the engine, and then he drives down the highway, heading out of town. We're in South Carolina right now, so even though it's February, the air is warm and the humidity makes my skin sticky, especially because we have the windows down. The ocean's pretty close by, the sand is golden, the sky is blue, and it makes my hands itch for the pencil and sketchbook Micha has in his lap.

When he finally stops the car, we're parked in front of a field covered in luscious grass and bushes. There's also this lofty tree in the center, by itself, some of the branches stretching toward the sky and others drooping toward the ground. It kind of reminds me of the tree back at home for some reason and it dawns on me why he might have brought me here.

Micha grins as he slips the key out of the ignition. "So when you said you wanted to come on the road with me, you said you'd love to spend your time drawing things that mean something to you, along with that tree I always used to climb up to get to you. Well, since that very meaningful tree is far, far away right now, I thought maybe you could draw this." He gestures at the field. "I found this field the other day when I was driving back from practice, searching for something that you could draw because I know you've been wanting to do a meaningful landscape drawing. The tree kind

299

of reminded me of the one back home, at least I think so, but then again I'm no artist." He pauses, waiting eagerly for my response.

I think I might have fallen in love with him even more. I didn't think that was possible, but every day the love I have for Micha grows stronger, especially when he does stuff like this for me.

I lean over the console toward him. "I love you," I say, unable to help myself. "And I love the tree."

"I love you, too," he says and then he kisses me. By the time we stop for air, we're both breathless and I've managed to climb over the console and onto his lap and his shirt's unbuttoned…I don't even know how it happened.

His hands are under my dress, grabbing at my flesh as he stares at me a little dazed. "So are you going to draw the tree?"

"Of course, but after I draw you first," I say. "Because you mean more to me than anything else in the world."

"But don't you have a ton of drawings of me already?"

"Yeah, but I don't have one with you sitting under this tree."

"You have to be tired of drawing me, though."

I shake my head. "No way. I will never get tired of you. Ever."

"No matter how many times you say that, I will never get tired of hearing it," he admits, and then a thoughtful expression rises on his face "So me under the tree, huh? That's your meaningful drawing?"

"I think it is," I say, and then we kiss for a little bit longer before we climb out of the car and walk toward the tree, happy, peaceful, and content as we live out our forever just how we want to—together.

If you loved

The Secret of Ella and Micha

have you read the first book in the

Breaking Nova **series?**

Find out how it all began in

Breaking Nova . . .

Prologue

Nova

Sometimes I wonder if there are some memories the mind doesn't want to deal with and that if it really wants to, it can block out the images, shut down, numb the pain connected to what we saw—what we didn't want to see. If we allow it to, the numbness can drown out everything, even the spark of life inside us. And eventually the person we once were is nothing but a vanishing memory.

I didn't always used to think this way. I used to have hope. I used to believe in things. Like when my father told me if I wanted something bad enough that I could make it happen.

"No one else in the world can make things happen for you, Nova," he'd said while we were lying on our backs on the hill in our backyard, staring up at the stars. I was six and happy and a little naïve, eating his words up like handfuls of sugar. "But if you want something bad enough and are willing to work hard at it, then anything's possible."

"Anything?" I'd said, turning my head toward him. "Even if I want to be a princess?"

He smiled, looking genuinely happy. "Even a princess."

I grinned, looking up at the sky, thinking how wonderful it would be to wear a diamond tiara on my head and a sparkly pink dress and matching heels. I would spin around in circles and laugh as my dress spun with me. Never once did I think about what it truly meant to be a princess and how impossible it was for me to actually become one.

"Earth to Nova." My boyfriend, Landon Evans, waves his hand in front of my face.

I blink my gaze away from the stars and angle my head sideways along the bottom of the grassy hill in his backyard, looking him in the eyes. "What's up?"

He laughs at me, but his smile looks unnatural, like it doesn't belong there. But that's normal for Landon. He's an artist, and he tells me that in order to portray pain in his portraits he has to carry it within him all the time. "You were totally spacing off on me there." The front porch light is on, and the fluorescent glow makes his honey-brown eyes look like the charcoal he uses for his sketchings.

I roll on my side and tuck my hands underneath my head, so I can really look at him. "Sorry, I was just thinking."

"You have that look on your face, like you're thinking deep." He rotates on his hip and props his elbow up on the ground, resting his head against his palm. Wisps of his inky-black hair fall into his eyes. "Want to talk about it?"

I shake my head. "No, I don't really feel like talking."

He offers me a trivial but genuine smile, and the sadness in my mind fleetingly dissolves. It's one of the things that I love about Landon. He's the only person on this planet who can make me smile—except for my dad, but he's no longer alive anymore, so smiles are rare in my book.

Landon and I were best friends up until about six months ago, and maybe that's why he can make me happy. We got to bond on a deeper level and understand each other before all the kissing and hormones came along. I know we're only eighteen and haven't even graduated high school yet, but sometimes, when I'm alone in my room, I can picture him and me together years ahead, in love, maybe getting married. It's surprising because for a long time after my dad died, I couldn't picture my future—I didn't want to. But things change. People evolve. Move on. Grow as new people enter their lives.

"I saw the picture you drew for the art project," I say, brushing some of the hair out of his eyes. "It was hanging up on Mr. Felmon's wall."

He frowns, which he always does whenever we're talking about his art. "Yeah, it didn't turn out how I planned."

"It seemed like you were sad when you were drawing it," I tell him, lowering my hand to my hip. "But all your drawings do."

Any happiness in his expression withers as he rolls onto his back and pinpoints his attention to the star-cut sky. He's silent for a while and I turn onto my back, letting him be, knowing that he's stuck in his own head. Landon is one of the saddest people I've met, and it's part of what drew me to him.

I was thirteen, and he'd just moved in across the street from me. He was sitting against the tree in his front yard, scribbling in a sketchbook, when I first saw him and decided to go over and introduce myself. It was right after my dad had died, and I'd pretty much kept my distance from people. But with Landon, I don't know, there was just something about him.

I'd crossed the street, very curious about what he was drawing. When I stopped in front of him, he glanced up at me, and I was taken aback by how much anguish was in his honey-brown eyes—the torture and internal suffering. I'd never seen so much of it in anyone my age before, and even though I didn't know what was causing it, I guessed we were going to be friends. He looked how I felt inside, like I'd been broken apart and the pieces hadn't healed correctly. Just like I guessed, we did become best friends—more than best friends, actually. We're almost inseparable, addicted to each other, and I absolutely hate being away from him because I feel lost and misplaced in the world whenever he's gone.

"Do you ever get the feeling that we're all just lost?" Landon utters, jerking me away from my thoughts again. "Just roaming around the earth, waiting around to die."

I bite on my lip, considering what he said as I find Cassiopeia in the sky. "Is that what you really think?"

"I'm not sure," he answers, and I turn my head, analyzing his perfect profile. "I sometimes wonder, though, what the point of life is." He stops, and it feels like he's waiting for me to say something.

"I'm not sure." I rack my brain for something else to add. But I can't think of a single coherent, reasonable response to his dark thoughts on the meaning of life, so I add, "I love you."

"I love you too, Nova," he promises without looking at me, then he reaches across the grass and grabs my hand, twining his fingers through mine. "And I mean that, Nova, no matter what. I love you."

We get lost in the stillness of the night while we watch the stars glimmer and fade. It's peaceful but unsettling at the same time, because I can't turn my thoughts off. I worry about him when he gets depressed like this. It's like he goes into his own little world that's carved of gloomy thoughts and a blackened future, and I can't reach him no matter how hard I try.

We lie quietly, watching the stars and holding on to each other. Eventually, I drift to sleep with my face pressed against the cool grass, the spring breeze chilly against my skin, and Landon's fingers soothingly stroking the inside of my wrist. When I wake up again, all the stars have blended in with the grayness of morning, the moon is tucked away in the glow of daybreak, and the grass is damp with dew. The first thing I notice is that Landon's hand is missing from mine, and it makes me feel empty, like one of my arms has been detached from my body.

I sit up, rubbing my eyes then stretching my arms

310

above my head as I glance around the backyard, searching for Landon. The only thing I can think of is that he got up to go to the bathroom, because he would never leave me sleeping on the hill alone in his backyard.

I push to my feet and brush the grass off the back of my legs before hiking up the hill toward his two-story house at the top of the backyard. It seems like a really long walk, because I'm tired—it's too early in the morning to be up. When I reach the back porch, I take my phone from my pocket to text Landon and see what he's doing. But I notice the back door is cracked, and I find myself walking inside, which is a little out of character for me. It's not like I'm used to walking into his house without being let in. I always knock, even when he texts me and tells me to come straight up to his room.

But this time, something begs my feet to step over the threshold. It's cold inside the kitchen, and I wonder how long the back door has been open. Shivering, I wrap my arms around myself and cross the entryway to the kitchen. Landon's parents are asleep upstairs, so I make sure to walk quietly, heading downstairs to Landon's room, which is in the basement. The stairs creak underneath my shoes, and I hold my breath the entire way down, not sure what will happen if his parents wake up and catch me sneaking down to his room.

"Landon," I whisper as I walk toward his bedroom. It's dark, except for the spark of the sunlight through the windows. "Are you down here?"

Silence is the only answer, and I almost turn around and go back upstairs. But then I hear the lyrics of an unknown song playing softly from somewhere in the house. I head for his bedroom door, and the music gets louder.

"Landon," I say as I approach his closed door, my nerves bubbling inside me. I don't know why I feel nervous. Or maybe I do. Maybe I've known for a long time, but I never wanted to accept it.

My hand trembles as I turn the knob. When I push the door open, every single word Landon's ever said to me suddenly makes sense to me. As the powerful lyrics playing from the stereo wrap around me, so does an undying chill. My hand falls lifeless to my side and I stand in the doorway, unblinking. I keep wishing for what I'm seeing to go away, to disappear from my mind, to erase the memories. I wish and wish— *will* it to happen—telling myself that if I want it badly enough, it'll happen. I start to count backward, focusing on the pattern and rhythm of the numbers, and after a few minutes, numbness swallows my heart. Just like I wanted, my surroundings fade and I can't feel anything.

I fall to the floor, hitting it hard, but I can't feel the pain...

Quinton

I'm driving way too fast. I know that and I know I should slow down, but everyone's complaining for me to hurry up and get them home. They're worried we're going to miss our curfew. Sometimes I wonder how I get myself into these kinds of messes. It's not like it's a big deal, but I'd probably be having a lot more fun if I was wasted with the rest of them, because it's spring break and I should be having fun. I'm not a fan of being the designated driver, but I usually end up offering to be one, and now I'm stuck driving around a bunch of drunken idiots.

"Stop smoking in here." I roll down the window as smoke begins to fill up the car. "My mom will smell it from a mile away, and then she's not going to let me drive her car anymore."

"Oh come on, Quinton," my girlfriend, Lexi, pouts as she takes a deep drag off her cigarette, then extends her arm out the open window. "We'll air it out."

Shaking my head, I reach over with my free hand

and snatch the cigarette from her. "No more smoking." I hold the cigarette out my cracked window until the cherry falls off, then release the rest out into the night. It's late, the road we're driving on is windy and curves around a lake, and we haven't seen a car in ages. It's good, though, since everyone else in the car is underage and drunk out of their minds.

Lexi sticks out her lip and crosses her arms over her chest, slumping back in her seat. "You're so boring when you're sober."

I press back a grin. We've been dating for a couple of years now, and she's the only girl I've ever been with and can ever see myself being with. I know it sounds superlame and cheesy because we're only eighteen, but I'm seriously going to end up marrying her.

Still pouting, she slides her hand up my thigh until she reaches my cock, then she gives it a good rub. "Does that feel good? Because I'll keep doing it if you just let me smoke."

I try not to laugh at her, because she's wasted and it'll probably piss her off, but it's funny how annoyed she's getting by my soberness. "And you're feisty and pouty when you're drunk." I squirm as she hits the right spot and fight not to shut my eyelids. "But I'm still not going to let you smoke in the car."

She rolls her eyes, draws her hand away from

me, and glances in the backseat, where my cousin Ryder is making out with some guy she met at the party. Their hands are all over each other. I'm not a fan of hanging out with her, but she comes out to Seattle sometimes and stays with my grandma. Lexi and Ryder became best friends during one of her visits when they were about twelve, and they've been inseparable ever since, which is pretty much how I met Lexi.

When Lexi looks away, her nose is scrunched. "So gross."

I decelerate the car for a sharp corner in the road. "Oh, don't pretend like you don't wish it was you and me back there." I wink at her and she rolls her eyes. "You know you do."

She sighs and lets her arms fall to her lap. "Yeah, right. If we were back there and I was trying to stick my tongue down your throat, you'd totally be like"— she makes air quotes—"'Lexi, please, there are people in the front seat who can see us.'"

"You're making me sound like an old man." I flash a playful grin at her as I downshift the car and the engine roars. The road is getting windier, and I have to slow down.

"You kind of are."

"Bullshit. I'm fucking fun as hell."

"No, you're nice as hell, Quinton Carter. You're seriously like the nicest guy I know, but the most fun? I'm not sure..." A conniving look crosses her face as she taps her finger against her lip. "How about we find out?" Without taking her eyes off me, she rolls the window down the rest of the way. The wind howls inside and blows her hair into her face.

"What the hell?" Ryder says from the backseat, jerking her lips away from the guy's, and plucks strands of her hair out of her mouth. "Lexi, roll up the damn window. I'm eating my own hair here."

"So Mr. Fucking Fun as Hell," Lexi says, with her eyes on me as she arches her back and moves her head toward the window. "Let's find out just how fun you are."

I don't like where she's going with this. She's too drunk, and even sober she's always been a daredevil, impulsive and a little bit reckless. "Lexi, what are you doing? Get in here. I don't want you to get hurt."

A lazy smile spreads across her lips as she sticks her head farther out the window. The pale glow of the moon hits her chest and makes her skin look ghostly against the darkness. "I want to see just how fun you are, Quinton." She extends her arms above her head as she slides up onto the windowsill. "I want to see how much you love me."

"Quinton, make her stop," Ryder says, scooting forward in the seat. "She's going to hurt herself."

"Lexi, stop it," I warn, gripping onto the steering wheel with one hand and reaching for her with my other. "I love you and that's why I need you to get down. *Right now.*"

She shakes her head. I can't see her face or if she's not holding onto anything. I have no idea what the hell she's doing or thinking, and I'm pretty sure she doesn't, either, and it's fucking terrifying.

"If you're so fun, then just let me be free," she calls out. Her dress is blowing up over her legs and her feet are tucked down between the seat and the door.

Ryder lifts her leg to climb over into the front seat, but smacks her head on the roof and falls back. Shaking my head, I gently tap on the brakes as I lean over in the seat to grab Lexi. My fingers snag the bottom of Lexi's dress and that's when I hear the scream. Seconds later, the car is spinning out of control, and I don't know what's up or what's down. Shards of glass fly everywhere and cut at my arms and face as I try to hold onto Lexi's dress. But I feel the fabric leave my fingers as I'm jarred to the side. Everyone is screaming and crying as metal crunches and bends. I see bright lights, feel the warmth of blood as something slashes through my chest.

"Quinton...," I hear someone whisper, but I can't see who it is. I try to open my eyes, but it feels like they're already open, yet all I see is darkness.

But maybe that's better than seeing what's actually there...